Defeat -of the- Ghost Riders

Trailblazer Books

HISTORIC CHARACTERS	TITLE
Gladys Aylward	Flight of the Fugitives
Mary McLeod Bethune	Defeat of the Ghost Riders
William & Catherine Booth	Kidnapped by River Rats
Charles Loring Brace	Roundup of the Street Rovers
William Bradford	The Mayflower Secret
John Bunyan	Traitor in the Tower
Amy Carmichael	The Hidden Jewel
Peter Cartwright	Abandoned on the Wild Frontier
Maude Cary	Risking the Forbidden Game
George Washington Carver	The Forty-Acre Swindle
Frederick Douglass	Caught in the Rebel Camp
Elizabeth Fry	The Thieves of Tyburn Square
Chief Spokane Garry	Exiled to the Red River
Barbrooke Grubb	Ambushed in Jaguar Swamp
Jonathan & Rosalind Goforth	Mask of the Wolf Boy
Sheldon Jackson	The Gold Miners' Rescue
Adoniram & Ann Judson	Imprisoned in the Golden City
Festo Kivengere	Assassins in the Cathedral
David Livingstone	Escape From the Slave Traders
Martin Luther	Spy for the Night Riders
Dwight L. Moody	Danger on the Flying Trapeze
Lottie Moon	Drawn by a China Moon
Samuel Morris	Quest for the Lost Prince
George Müller	The Bandit of Ashley Downs
John Newton	The Runaway's Revenge
Florence Nightingale	The Drummer Boy's Battle
John G. Paton	Sinking the Dayspring
William Penn	Hostage on the Nighthawk
Joy Ridderhof	Race for the Record
Nate Saint	The Fate of the Yellow Woodbee
Rómulo Sauñe	Blinded by the Shining Path
William Seymour	Journey to the End of the Earth
Menno Simons	The Betrayer's Fortune
Mary Slessor	Trial by Poison
Hudson Taylor	Shanghaied to China
Harriet Tubman	Listen for the Whippoorwill
William Tyndale	The Queen's Smuggler
John Wesley	The Chimney Sweep's Ransom
Marcus & Narcissa Whitman	Attack in the Rye Grass
David Zeisberger	The Warrior's Challenge

Defeat -of the- Ghost Riders

Dave & Neta Jackson

Illustrated by Julian Jackson

Evanston, Illinois 60202

Published by Castle Rock Creative, Inc.
Evanston, Illinois 60202

Previously published by
Bethany House, a division of
Baker Publishing Group

Unless otherwise noted, all Scripture quotations are from the King James Version of the Bible

Inside illustrations by Julian Jackson
Cover illustration by Catherine Reishus McLaughlin

ISBN: 978-1-939445-25-4

Printed in the United States of America

For a complete listing of
books by Dave and Neta Jackson visit
www.daveneta.com
www.trailblazerbooks.com

The historical events referred to in this book are all based on fact. Celeste Key and her family and their involvement in these events, however, are entirely fictional.

The Statesboro riot, the "five little girls" who made up the first school, the student who had appendicitis, the quarry explosion, and the treatment of some black soldiers when they returned home to the South from World War I (and II) are facts woven into the story of our fictional family.

Events involving Mrs. Bethune approximate the historical time line, with a few minor exceptions. For instance, Dr. Madison Mason visited Mrs. Bethune's school and took the injured Mrs. Bethune to Chicago in 1906 when the school had been in existence for two years, instead of just one year as the story implies. It has not always been possible to follow the exact time line of events, since different biographies are inexact about "what happened when."

Dave and Neta Jackson, husband and wife writing team, are the authors or coauthors of more than 120 books that have sold over 2.5 million copies. They are best known for the 40-volume Trailblazer Books series for young readers and the Hero Tales series for families. Adults love their Yada Yada Prayer Group series, House of Hope series, Harry Bentley series, and Windy City Neighbors series along with numerous nonfiction books. They make their home in the Chicago area. Find out more about them at www.daveneta.com.

CONTENTS

Chapter 1

Fire in the Night

CELESTE STAMPED A BROWN BARE FOOT and tightened her grip on her jumping rope. "Why can't I go out to play?" she demanded crossly. "I took care of Button all mornin' for Mama. You're just mean, Papa, that's what!"

The Key family was finishing their noon meal of greens, fried mush, and sorghum syrup in the small clapboard house on Peachtree Street. The sweltering day that August of 1904 lay like a heavy blanket over Statesboro, Georgia, stuffing every corner of the little house. But Samuel Key had just announced that the "young'uns" had to stay inside the rest of the day. The other children—Tom, fifteen; Lucy, twelve; and Buddy, six—eyed their

father to see how he was going to react to this mutiny on the part of eight-year-old Celeste.

But Samuel just frowned, pushed back his chair, and pulled on his cap. Tom jumped up and grabbed his own cap, ready to go back to the blacksmith shop with his father to finish the work they'd started that morning.

KEY'S BLACKSMITHY said the blue and red sign over the wide stable door. The whole family was proud of that sign. *Their* papa didn't work for nobody, white or black. Samuel Key owned his own blacksmith shop, and business was good. A few rich people owned those newfangled motorcars—"horseless carriages" they were called—but most people still relied on horses for everyday business. Even some of the white folks in Statesboro came to Key's Blacksmithy to get their horses shod or their harnesses repaired.

But Samuel turned at the door, his face troubled. "No, Tom," he said. "I want you to help your mother this afternoon. She's gotta deliver laundry 'cross town."

"Aw, Papa!" groaned Tom. "Why can't Lucy and Buddy—?"

"Don't argue with me, boy," snapped Samuel. "It's you I need to go with your mother today. Do those deliveries and git your mother back here soon's you can."

His eyes swept the rest of the children and finally rested on Celeste. The little girl's lip was stuck out in a pout, and her arms were crossed stubbornly.

"Trouble's a'brewin'," he said darkly. "I'm sayin' it again. Don't want none of the rest of you young'uns to go outside today." Celeste squirmed under his piercing gaze. "You hear me, missy?"

Celeste nodded and hung her head. But as the door rattled shut, her lip stuck out even farther. What did Papa mean by trouble? She couldn't get in trouble just playing with her jumping rope out back of the house.

✧ ✧ ✧ ✧

Mama and Tom had been gone for an hour, lugging a heavy basket between them with clean, starched clothes. They had to make deliveries to two of Mama's clients—white folks over on Hill Street who hired Lilly Key to do their weekly laundry.

Doing laundry for other folks was a backbreaking job. First, Lilly scrubbed the clothes on a washboard with hard soap, then boiled them with soft soap in a big kettle over a fire in the backyard. Buddy was then put to work lifting the clothes with a large wooden "fork" into the rinse water—white things got another rinse with a bleaching agent—then fed through a crank ringer to squeeze the water out. Finally, Lilly and Lucy hung the clothes on the old clotheslines to dry in the hot Georgia breeze, then folded them carefully in a basket and returned them to their owners.

"At least these white folks have maids who can do the ironin'!" Mama always said gratefully, stretching the sore muscles in her back and shoulders. And the money she got paid always went in the rusty coffee can to help put food on the table.

Now the house was quiet, except for the occasional drone of a fly against a windowpane. Celeste gave one last rock to the cradle Papa had made. Button's chubby arms and legs were flung out in peaceful slumber. Tiptoeing to the door of the room her parents and Button slept in, Celeste peeked around the curtain into the main room. No sign of Buddy; he must have fallen asleep in the back room shared by all four children. Lucy had her back to Celeste, humming to herself as she cleaned out the ashes from the woodburning cookstove at the far end of the main room, which the Key family used for cooking, eating, and sitting.

Celeste's jumping rope lay waiting by the door, which Lucy had opened to catch any little breeze. She moved quietly across the scrubbed wood floor, silently picked up the rope, and slipped outside.

She wanted to whoop with joy but only twirled around in a little dance. What a relief to get out of that stuffy house! The sun still hung high in the afternoon sky, but a light breeze ruffled the tops of the big oaks lining Peachtree Street, where colored folks like themselves lived. Papa's blacksmith shop was just down the unpaved street and around the corner.

Skipping across the dirt street, Celeste put a fat oak between herself and the little clapboard house. Now Lucy couldn't see her and haul her back inside.

In fact, Celeste reasoned to herself, if she went one street over, Lucy wouldn't see her at all and she could play all afternoon.

As Celeste lost sight of her house, she thought, *Where is everybody?* The streets seemed strangely deserted. Well, all the better for her. No one to make mention to Mama or Papa that they'd seen her playing outside that afternoon.

Feeling safe from discovery, Celeste twirled her rope and tried to jump like Lucy had taught her. But her feet kept getting tangled up in the rope. Finally, bored and hot, she wandered, dragging the rope behind her. She'd never walked around their neighborhood all by herself before. Passing house after house and turning on this street and that gave her a feeling of grown-up importance. She'd just walk awhile, then head back before Mama and Tom got home.

But finally her legs felt tired. Celeste sat down against a big oak, feeling the rough, warm bark on her back. Within moments she was fast asleep.

She awoke with a start. The sun was gone, and twilight hung over the trees. *I've got to get home!* she thought, starting to run. But finding Peachtree Street again wasn't as easy as she thought. Anxious, Celeste ran faster. She wanted to ask someone where Peachtree Street was, but she didn't see anyone she knew, and one old man just shouted at her, "Git on home, girl—be quick about it!"

Then somewhere up ahead, Celeste heard people shouting. She ran toward the sound; surely *someone* could tell her where Peachtree Street was. But as she came to a corner and looked down the next street, she hesitated. The people she saw were white and there were a lot of them. She quickly darted behind a tree. What were they all doing in the colored neighborhood?

Still, Celeste pondered, maybe one of these white people could tell her how to find Peachtree. After all, the people Mama did laundry for seemed nice enough. And Mr. Gunderson at Gunderson's Mercantile where Mama bought cloth to make britches and dresses always gave her a lollipop. But... these white people seemed angry. Even more strange, some of them were wearing white sheets over their heads, like they'd just rolled out of bed.

She giggled at the ridiculous costume—but just then the shouting got louder, and suddenly several torches flared. "Key's Blacksmithy!" somebody yelled. "Teach these blacks not to mess with white folks!"

The crowd surged past Celeste's bushy hiding place. She felt a rush of both hope and terror. Those people were going to her papa's blacksmith shop! If she followed them, she would find her way home. But why were they going there? What were they going to do?

Her legs felt leaden with fear. But somehow she managed to put one foot in front of the other and creep along behind the trees and bushes lining the street, following the crowd. And sure enough—soon she saw the blue and red sign of Papa's shop! Now if she could only get past without Papa seeing her and sneak back into the house....

Suddenly, she saw a torch flying through the blue-black dusk, landing on a pile of straw bales stacked on the side of the blacksmith shop. Another torch was flung through the opening to the loft where hay was stored to feed Willy, Papa's mule, and the horses who were brought each day to get horseshoes fitted. In seconds, flames were leaping from the loft and up the side of the blacksmith shop.

Celeste screamed, but it was lost in the ugly laughter of the mob, who cheered as the flames lept higher. Then, like a restless, hungry cat on the prowl, the crowd suddenly took off running down the street, as if looking for another unsuspecting victim.

A dark figure appeared in the doorway of the blacksmithy, coughing and tugging on a rope. It was Papa! He was leading Willy the mule out into the fresh air. The mule's ears were laid back, and he was squealing with fright. Slapping the mule on the rump, Samuel Key grabbed a burlap bag, plunged it into the water barrel beside the door, and started slapping the flames.

The mule bolted past Celeste, his eyes ringed white with panic. Fear rooted Celeste to the ground. She wanted to run to her father, but she was afraid of the fire. And what if he got angry with her for leaving the house?

Just then another figure—smaller and boyish—came running down the street. "Papa! Papa! Come quick!" Buddy screamed. "They got Tom!"

Celeste saw her father look helplessly at the flames licking hungrily at the wooden blacksmith

shop. Then with a howl of desperation, the big man tossed aside the wet burlap sack and took off running after Buddy.

✧ ✧ ✧ ✧

Celeste crept up to the little clapboard house on Peachtree Street, her teeth chattering even in the muggy evening. The door was closed, but she could hear anxious voices through the open window—Lucy's and Mama's. Button was whimpering. Where was Papa? Was he inside? Oh, how she longed to be safe inside the house with her family! But did she dare go back inside? Were they all angry at her?

Tears spilled down the little girl's cheeks. Why, oh, why did she disobey her papa and run away this afternoon?

Lucy's high-pitched wail carried out the window. "But *why* did they attack you, Mama?"

Celeste heard her mother moan. "I... I don't know. Something to do with that murder trial goin' on at the courthouse—two colored fellows are accused of killing a white family. Everyone's goin' crazy! As Tom and I got done deliverin' the laundry, a group of white boys started yelling at us, calling us names, telling us to get out of their neighborhood. I begged Tom to ignore them, but he... he yelled back at them, told them we had business there. That made them mad. Before I knew what was happening, the boys had pushed me down and were beating on Tom." Lilly started to cry.

"Mama, I'm scared!" It was Buddy's voice, pushing in anxiously. "Will Papa find Tom?"

The sobs and moans increased. "Oh, God, I hope so. But now Celeste is missin', too! And that mob—burnin' your papa's shop. Oh, Lord, oh, Lord, what we gonna do?"

Celeste couldn't bear it anymore. She burst into the room and flung herself into her mother's arms. "Here I am, Mama!" she cried. "I only went outside to play with my jumpin' rope, an' I . . . I got lost."

Jumping rope. Celeste suddenly realized her hands were empty. "My jumping rope be lost, too," she said mournfully.

To her surprise, her mother hugged her fiercely, kissing her all over her dirt-streaked face. Then, just as suddenly, Lilly held Celeste at arm's length and scolded, "You naughty girl! Didn't you hear your papa tell you there was trouble in the town? Ain't we got enough to worry about right now without you runnin' off and scarin' me half to death? I'm a'gonna switch your legs good—"

"Mama!" screeched Buddy, who was peering out a window. "Here comes Papa! He's got Tom!"

Celeste's switching was forgotten as Lilly flew to the door and opened it wide. Samuel Key stumbled in, carrying lanky Tom in his big arms. The teenager's face was swollen and bloody, his clothes torn and dirty.

"He ain't dead," Samuel grunted, laying the boy down gently, "an' I don't think nothin's broke—'cept maybe a couple of ribs." Samuel's face was twisted with grief and anger. "Should never have let you two go this afternoon," he mumbled. "Not with that murder trial making everyone crazy."

The other children crowded close, staring in shock at their older brother lying unconscious on the bed. But Lilly was already a whirlwind of activity—wringing out a wet rag and beginning to wash Tom's bloody face, all the while snapping out instructions. "Lucy, put some water on to boil and tear up those clean rags for bandages. Buddy, find the iodine. Samuel, help me get these torn clothes off him."

Celeste crept over to the bed she shared with Lucy and curled up in a little ball. Mama wasn't going to switch her, after all, she thought with guilty relief. Her tummy growled with hunger, but the little girl's eyelids began to droop as her mother cleaned and bandaged Tom's wounds with a singsong voice.

"There, there, Tommy boy... Lord's gonna see us through.... It's gonna be all right.... Mama gonna take care of you.... You sleep, now, sleep...."

Chapter 2

Skin Black as Midnight

THE NEXT MORNING the whole Key family—except Tom—stood looking dismally at the pile of charred wood and ashes that used to be Key's Blacksmithy. Tears glistened on Lilly Key's face as she held baby Button on her hip and stared at the ruins. Samuel kicked away some of the still-smoldering wood and bent down to pick up a pair of iron tongs and a heavy hammer. His jaw was set tightly.

Celeste, pressed close to her mother, felt her take a deep breath. "The family's still together, Samuel," the slightly built woman said bravely. "That's the important thing. And Tom's gonna mend in a week or two. We can build the blacksmith shop again, start over—"

"No." Samuel cut her off gruffly. "We can't start over again—not here." The tall, muscular man took three big strides to stand in front of his wife. He lowered his voice and whispered fiercely, "Don't you understand, Lilly? The white folks is all stirred up. They ain't gonna let us start over again. They don't want no Negroes to make good in Georgia. They just lookin' for an excuse to beat us down, and they found their excuse when those two black fellows was accused of killing that white family. Won't be no time at all 'afore the Ku Klux Klan be ridin' again, beatin' and terrorizin' colored folks."

Celeste pressed closer to her mother. She didn't understand what Papa was talking about, but the tone of his voice frightened her. Papa sounded scared.

Samuel looked away from his wife's face and stared once again at the charred ruins. "Klan don't want us here. Well, I got the message," he said. "We gotta get out of Statesboro—get out of Georgia if we can."

"But, Samuel," said Lilly, her voice quavering, "we ain't got no place to go."

Button squealed and waved a chubby arm. A man was coming toward them leading a mule.

"It's Willy!" Buddy yelped and ran over to stroke the big bay mule's velvety nose.

"'Preciate you returning my mule, Clay," Samuel said. "Thought I'd lost him for sure."

The neighbor handed Willy's lead rope to Samuel

without smiling. His eyes darted nervously this way and that, as if worried about being seen. Then he leaned close to Samuel. "Florida," he said huskily. "Some rich guy named Flagler is building a railroad down the east coast of Florida. Needs workers—lots of workers. Soon as I can get my family packed up, I'm getting out of here." The man jerked his head at the smoking remains of Key's Blacksmithy. "And if I were you, Key, I'd pack up your missus and your young'uns behind that mule and head for Florida, too."

✧ ✧ ✧ ✧

Celeste was tired of riding in the wagon. She was hot and thirsty and crowded. Rolled-up mattresses, barrels with dishes packed in sawdust, chairs, cooking pots, and bundles of clothes all tied down in the wagon bed made it hard to find a comfortable place to sit. Papa, Mama, and baby Button rode on the wagon seat as Willy plodded slowly day after day, heading south toward Florida. At night they found a place along Georgia's red dirt roads to camp, back in the trees, out of sight. But during the day the sun shone relentlessly.

"Quit kicking me, Celeste," complained Tom, whose lanky frame was propped against one of the mattresses. "Don't you know I got some ribs broke?"

"Didn't kick you," pouted Celeste. "You just too big, take up too much room. I gotta have some room for *my* feet, too." And she gave another shove with her bare feet.

"Keep your feet to yourself, Celeste Key," scolded Mother, half turning on the wagon seat. "Samuel," she said, turning back to her husband, "we've gotta get water soon. The children—"

"I know, I know, Lilly," said Samuel. His voice was tired. "Palatka just be another five miles. That's where we cross the St. John's River. We can fill up our water jars there."

They'd been on the road ten days. They had tried to leave Statesboro in the early dawn, before the townspeople were awake. But those who were up and about stared at the heavily loaded wagon and whispered among themselves. A few whites laughed and jeered, "Good riddance!" Samuel had sternly instructed the children, no matter what happened, to avoid eye contact and keep their mouths shut.

Once on the road, however, the children began to feel excited. They'd lived in Statesboro their whole lives; now they were moving to Florida! A work camp for Flagler's railroad was growing up at Daytona—right on the ocean!

But the excitement had gradually withered as one long, slow, dusty day turned into another. Now everyone just felt cranky and hot. After crossing the state line into Florida a few days earlier, they began to see other black families like themselves, wagons piled high, heading south to work on the railroad.

Celeste saw kids in the other wagons. She wanted to get down and run and jump and play. But Papa had said no. Everyone had to stay on the wagon. He didn't want a child falling under a wagon wheel or

getting stepped on by a mule. Pouting, Celeste stuck out her lip and glared at Buddy, who was riding easily on top of a mattress.

"Mama," tattled Buddy, "Celeste stuck her tongue out at me."

"Did not!"

"Did so!"

"Stop it!" Papa thundered. "Don't want to hear one more peep till we get to the river."

Celeste heaved a big sigh. She was going to scream if she had to ride in this wagon one more minute! Kicking her heels over the side of the wagon, she wondered whether the river was shallow and they'd just drive across, or whether Willy would have to swim with the wagon floating behind him.

Finally she felt the wagon begin the gentle descent to the river crossing, then heard Papa's big voice, "Whoa! Whoa there, Willy." He gave a low whistle. "Look at that, Lilly. Must be seven wagons already waitin' to cross."

Samuel Key climbed down the wagon wheel and handed the reins to his wife. "Be back as soon as I find out what's what," he said, then disappeared among the other wagons.

Lilly sighed. "Come on, kids, let's at least wait in the shade of that tree. Tom, can you get down all right? Lucy, you and Buddy get those water jars and come with me—see if we can find some water to drink. Celeste, you take Button and wait with Tom—Celeste?... Celeste! Now, where did that girl disappear to?"

Celeste had not waited to hear her mother's commands. The moment her father was hidden from sight among the other wagons, she had slipped over the side and flew away in the opposite direction. She wasn't going to stay in that wagon one more second! And besides, the river looked cool and wet and inviting.

The little girl's bare feet scurried over the cool grass as she ran in a wide curve around the bunched-up wagons and down toward the river. But as she neared the water's edge a little downriver from the waiting wagon teams, she stopped short. A strange-looking, flat-bottomed boat was steaming straight toward the bank. It had two paddle wheels, one on each side, and on one side was a little square "house" with a smokestack puffing.

Celeste's eyes widened. Was the boat going to crash right into the riverbank?

But the boat blew a whistle and the paddle wheels slowed, then turned backward as the boat slid neatly up to a wide wooden dock sticking out into the river. Celeste watched, fascinated, as first one, then another wagon drove out on the dock and down a wide plank onto the flat deck of the ferry. This took a long time, with men putting blocks of wood in front and back of each wagon wheel and calming the jittery mules.

Finally the boat blew its whistle, the smokestack puffed, the paddles began turning, and the ferry churned away from the dock and headed across the St. John's River with the two wagons on board.

With a start, Celeste realized she'd been gone from their own wagon a long time. *Oh no*, she thought. I'm in big trouble now.

She ran back the way she had come, looking for Willy and the wagon. A quick glance showed her that Papa wasn't back yet—good! But Mama was pacing up and down beside the wagon, and she looked plenty angry.

Just then Celeste saw a young colored woman in a dark blue cotton dress approach her mother. The stranger didn't look like one of the travelers; her dress was too neat and clean. In one hand she held a parasol to keep off the hot sun; in the other she held the hand of a small boy about four years old. The woman held her head erect, making her look tall and regal.

Celeste slipped around to the far side of the wagon and pulled herself up the wagon wheel and onto the wagon bed.

From under the tree, Lucy saw her. "Mama—!" she called out and pointed. But Lilly just raised a hand to silence her eldest daughter. The stranger was speaking.

"Excuse me, I hope I'm not being too forward. But I was wondering where you folks are headed?" asked the woman politely. "I live in Palatka and saw all the wagons heading for the river."

"Why, down Daytona way," replied Lilly. She sounded pleased to be speaking to another woman. "We hear there's railroad work to be had, and my man, he..." Her voice trailed off.

"Oh yes, the Florida East Coast Railway," said the woman. Celeste peeked over a bundle and stared at her. The woman's skin was as black as midnight—not golden brown like the Key family—and her voice was silky and fine. Maybe, thought Celeste with a little giggle of excitement, maybe she was really an African princess in disguise.

"I'm a school teacher here in Palatka," the woman was saying, "and I noticed all the children. . . ." Her gaze swept over the wagons lined up waiting to cross the river. "Is there a school in Daytona for the children of railroad workers?"

Lilly seemed flustered. "A-a school? For colored children? Well, I don't rightly know, but they ain't never had one before, not even in Statesboro."

"Oh, Statesboro," said the woman, a sudden spark of understanding in her eyes. "I heard there was trouble there a few weeks back. Your family—?" She hesitated politely, and suddenly Lilly Key was pouring out their tale of woe to this woman with the kind voice—about the murder trial and the riot and the beating of Tom and the Ku Klux Klan burning Samuel Key's blacksmith shop and having to leave their home and livelihood for—

"What you doin', Lilly?" interrupted a stern voice. Samuel Key was striding back to the wagon, frowning. "Shouldn't be telling a stranger our business. Tom—Lucy—Buddy... back in the wagon with Celeste. Come on, now, Lilly—we gotta pull up to keep our place in line." Turning his back on the woman in the blue dress and helping Tom climb back into the wagon, Samuel firmly put an end to the conversation.

"You in one heap of trouble, girl," Lucy hissed to Celeste, but Celeste just stuck out her tongue.

As the reins slapped and the wagon lurched forward, Celeste glanced at the woman in blue and the boy watching them. The woman's eyes were direct and fearless, and suddenly Celeste felt like the woman could see deep down inside her. Quickly she lowered her eyes.

Then she put her hand over her mouth and giggled. That black-skinned woman had helped her out without even knowing it. By distracting her mother, Celeste was able to sneak back onto the wagon without getting caught!

Chapter 3

Shanty Town

"Did you get some customers, Mama?" Lucy asked eagerly as her mother ducked into the doorway of the shanty house and unpinned her hat.

"Any jobs at them new fancy hotels goin' up?" Tom wanted to know.

"Did you see the ocean, Mama?" asked Celeste, eyes wide.

Lilly Key smiled tiredly as she swooped Button from the floor and planted a kiss on his fat cheek. "No, I didn't see the ocean. That's on the peninsula across the Halifax River. Yes, I lined up three new customers starting next Monday—and one lady said lots of rich folks from the north

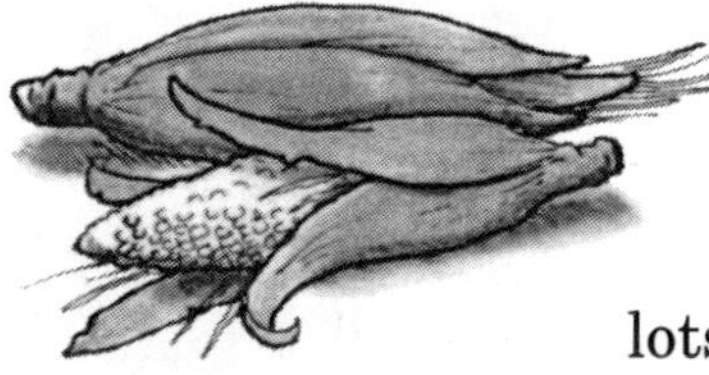

come in the winter months, so there'll be plenty of seasonal work if we can do it. But I'm gonna need help from all you young'uns."

"Mama," pleaded Tom, "what about hotel jobs for me?"

"Now, Tom, you know your papa wants you to sign on with the railroad work crew soon as your ribs heal. He don't hold with hobnobbing with those white folks more'n we can help it. I see you got the wood chopped.... Lucy, you got those beans started? Good... Celeste—how come you ain't got that corn shucked like I done asked you to?"

"'Cause she been playin' with that Lena next door," smirked Lucy. "Came home when she saw you a'comin'."

Celeste glared at her big sister.

"Girl, you know chores come first, playin' comes after," Mother said crossly. "I catch you doin' that again, you stuck in the house for a week. Now, you git a'shuckin' quick-like. Buddy, you help her so I can grind up some cornmeal."

"Aw, Mama, that ain't fair!" Buddy protested. "I already fetched the water like you asked me. How come I gotta help Celeste when she—?"

But Lilly had already bustled outside to stir the beans and salt pork bubbling in the pot over the open fire. They'd had to leave their cookstove behind in Statesboro, and it would be weeks before Samuel made enough money on the railroad to afford even a used one. They had already gone into debt to get materials to build the simple two-room shanty they were living in.

The Key family had been in Daytona nearly a month, and the September sea breezes had eased the muggy heat to a pleasant warmth. A shanty town for railroad workers and hotel builders was springing up on the western side of the railroad tracks. The village of Daytona—where the man named Flagler was building one of his fancy tourist hotels—was on the other side of the railroad tracks, along the banks of the Halifax River, which flowed south and into the sea. Between the river and the ocean was a peninsula of land where the homes of a few rich people looked out to the sea.

Every morning Samuel got up with the first light and caught the work train that took the large crew of men south to where new track was being laid on the railroad spurs. He didn't get home until after the young ones were in bed. *If* he came home, that is. Sometimes the crew worked late to finish a section and just slept on the ground, ready to start even earlier the next day.

The family had camped in the colored section, or Shanty Town as it was called, until Samuel and Tom had built a shanty. It was a far cry from the neat clapboard house with glass windows in Statesboro. "But it'll do till we get back on our feet," Lilly said encouragingly, trying not to see the bitter look in Samuel's eyes.

Celeste liked Florida—except for the big black bugs and lizards that seemed to crawl everywhere. Sitting outside the shanty with Buddy, she lazily pulled the husk off an ear of dried corn so that Mama could cut off the kernels and grind them into flour. There were a lot of children to play with in Shanty Town, and a new family seemed to arrive every day. Except, she frowned to herself, Mama and Papa didn't seem to believe in playing. Work, work, work—that's all they thought about. And she hadn't even seen the ocean yet.

"Hurry up, lazy bones," grumbled Buddy. "I'm shuckin' three ears to every one you do. An' it ain't even my job."

Celeste was just about to stick her tongue out at her brother when her mouth dropped open instead. Coming up the path to their shanty was a woman riding a bicycle who looked vaguely familiar. She was wearing a dark blue dress and bonnet, and her skin was as black as midnight.

It was the woman who had talked to Mama at the ferry crossing back in Palatka.

"Hello," smiled the woman, dismounting from the bicycle. "My name is Mrs. Bethune. Is your mother home?"

Celeste stared. *Mrs.* Bethune? Why, she'd never heard a black woman called by that title. She'd been taught to call white people "Mr. So-and-so" or "Mrs. So-and-so." But white people always called her mama and papa "Lilly" and "Samuel."

Buddy had already run inside the shanty and reappeared with his mother.

"Mrs. Key?" said the woman. "My name is Mrs. Bethune—Mary McLeod Bethune. I'm a teacher, and

I'm starting a school for girls right here in Daytona. I'd like to talk to you about letting your girls attend my school." Mrs. Bethune didn't look at Celeste, but the little girl had the feeling the woman was looking at her with eyes in the back of her head.

"A school?" said Lilly, wiping her hands on her apron. "For girls? Right here? Oh, my—" She put her hand to her cheek. "Why, I'm forgettin' my manners. Won't you come in and have something to drink?"

Lilly led the way into the little shanty. Forgetting her shucking job, Celeste tiptoed into the cool shadows, hoping her mother wouldn't notice.

"Wish it was lemonade," said Lilly apologetically, dipping two glasses of water from the drinking bucket and sitting down with her guest. "But we ain't had time to get settled—don't have no icebox yet."

"Water's just fine," said the woman graciously. "We've met before, haven't we? At the ferry crossing in Palatka—"

"That's right!" said Lilly, her eyes lighting up. "But... wasn't you a teacher in Palatka? Yet you're sayin' you're starting a school here." She shook her head. "Can't hardly see why. This be just a shanty town... people comin' and goin' all the time. Not even a real community."

Mrs. Bethune smiled. Her teeth were very white against her dark face. "But that's just it!" she beamed. "There are hundreds of children in this railroad camp. For a shanty town or any town to become a community, it needs churches and schools—something to draw the people together and give them a future."

Lilly Key shook her head again. "I don't know. My man and me... we didn't have no schoolin'. Jobs—that's what we need. Just to be left in peace so's we can work and put food on the table for our young'uns."

Mrs. Bethune's eyes shone with passion. "Jobs, of course, my dear woman. But our people need so much more! We need vision to see what the world is all about and hope that the future holds more than the past. And skills—skills to give us confidence that we can do anything! Anything we have a mind to do."

Lilly seemed transfixed.

"My school," the woman went on excitedly, "will give girls a classic education in grammar and literature, arithmetic and science, music and art. At the same time, by living at the school the girls will learn practical skills such as cooking and sewing and domestic arts." She leaned forward and touched Lilly on the arm. "Wouldn't you like that for your girls, Mrs. Key?"

"To think..." breathed Lilly, as if she'd just caught a glimpse of paradise. Then suddenly she frowned. "How much do it cost, Mrs. Bethune? Sounds like something only rich folks can afford."

Mrs. Bethune sat back in her chair. "Fifty cents a week per girl to help cover their upkeep."

Lilly sighed. "I 'preciate you thinking about our girls, Mrs. Bethune, but... I don't think so. Can't spare my Lucy. I take in laundry from white folks, an' she do most everything else. We just gettin' by."

"Then how about the younger one?" This time

Mrs. Bethune's keen eyes looked directly at Celeste.

"Celeste?" Lilly laughed nervously. "She be one heap of trouble, that one. Can't count on her for nothin'—Celeste! What you doin' standing there? Why ain't you outside shuckin' that corn? Lan'! It take you a month of Sundays to do one simple job."

Celeste scurried outside but heard her mother say, "See what I mean? That girl lazy from the inside out. Always running off playing. Don't pay no mind to what her papa and I say... got a mind of her own. No, that one don't deserve no schoolin'."

"On the contrary, Mrs. Key," Mrs. Bethune disagreed gently. "All the more reason to teach children like Celeste good manners and their duties as citizens. Please, think about it and talk to your husband. I'll come around in a few days and see what your answer is."

As the two women came outside, Lilly's curiosity got the best of her. "Uh, your husband be in town, too, Mrs. Bethune?"

A shadow seemed to pass over Mrs. Bethune's face and then was gone. "My husband is still teaching school in Palatka," she said quietly. "Little Albert and I hope he will be able to join us soon here in Daytona." She picked up her bicycle and with a wave was soon out of sight.

✧ ✧ ✧ ✧

Samuel Key was upset when he heard about the school. "White folks won't like it," he growled. "They'll

think we're getting uppity, forgettin' our place. That Bethune woman just gonna cause trouble for us."

It was late at night. The children were asleep on their mattresses in the sleeping room of the shanty, while Samuel wearily finished up the supper of corn bread and beans that Lilly had saved for him.

"But I've been thinking, Samuel," said Lilly. "Celeste be a handful, right? Frankly, she's not much help, havin' to run after her all the time. Sometimes it's easier just to do the chores myself. But that schoolteacher got a good head on her shoulders. Don't think she take any nonsense. Maybe staying at her school would pound some sense into Celeste's head."

"I don't know, Lilly... don't feel right turnin' to somebody else to solve our problems. We gotta hang tight as a family. Only way we gonna make it."

"But schoolin', Samuel... think on it. Only way things gonna change for us is if our young'uns get themselves some education, just like the white young'uns. Now here's a chance come knockin' at our very door."

Samuel pushed back his chair and rose wearily. "What's knockin' at our door is poverty, sure and certain, if I don't get Tom workin' on that railroad. He be mended enough. I'm takin' him tomorrow."

✧ ✧ ✧ ✧

Celeste was supposed to be gathering kindling in the scrub brush on the edge of Shanty Town, but she lay under the shade of a bush, squinting her eyes at the white puffy clouds and imagining they looked like rabbits or mules or dogs. It was Sunday—Papa's day off—and the shanty felt crowded and hot.

When she finally did come skipping up the path with her meager armful of dry branches, she saw a well-used bicycle leaning against the shanty.

"Had enough trouble in Statesboro," Papa was saying inside. "Don't have a mind to go round askin' for it down here in Daytona."

"I understand your feeling, Mr. Key," said a familiar female voice. *Mr*. Key, thought Celeste. Uh-huh. No one would call her papa mister except that teacher woman, Mrs. Bethune. "But," the woman's voice went on, "don't you think it's time we Negroes did something to better our condition instead of waiting for whites to allow it?"

There was silence from within the shanty... then the sound of a chair scraping. "Please, think about it," Mrs. Bethune pleaded. "If it's a matter of money, maybe we can provide a scholarship—"

"Ain't takin' no handouts," growled Samuel. "If we send our girl to your school, we be payin' ourselves."

Footsteps were coming to the door. Celeste scurried away. She didn't want to be caught eavesdropping. Maybe she should go find some more kindling.

From the safety of the nearby bushes, Celeste watched Mrs. Bethune get on her bicycle and ride out of sight among the other shanties. How come no one was asking *her* if she wanted to go to school? Celest thought to herself. "Sound like a lot of work to me," she muttered. "If that Bethune woman gets hold of me, when I ever gonna get over to the ocean and play on them beaches?"

Chapter 4

Head, Hand, and Heart

On the morning of October 3, 1904, Celeste trudged beside her mother, threading the dusty paths of Shanty Town on their way to Mrs. Bethune's school. Mama had remade one of Lucy's old dresses for her, and she carried a bundle with a second dress, a sweater, her nightgown, underthings, one pair of knitted socks, and a pair of hand-me-down shoes for cool weather—all rolled up in a flannel blanket. Celeste's hair was braided tight in four neat braids and wouldn't need redoing until she came home again on Sunday afternoon.

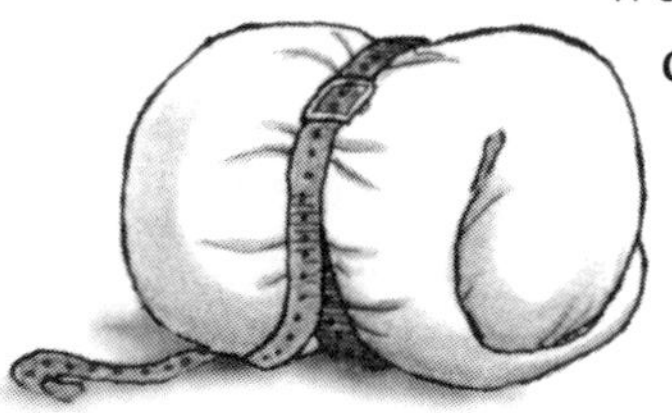

How far we have to walk, anyway? Celeste thought, scowling. *Don't need no book*

learning, anyhow. Her only satisfaction was remembering the wistful look on Lucy's face, standing in the doorway with baby Button on her hip. Lucy was jealous of her! With a toss of her head, Celeste had said sassily, "Well, I be off to school now!" and followed her mother down the path.

"Oak Street... this is it," murmured her mother at last as they heard the ringing of a hand bell. Mary McLeod Bethune was standing in the doorway of 529 Oak Street, beaming a welcome to several girls carrying bundles similar to Celeste's, who were also arriving with their mothers.

"Welcome to the Daytona Educational and Industrial School for Negro Girls!" Mrs. Bethune said joyously.

Celeste stared. It was just a house, and a sorry-looking one at that. Paint was peeling, the grass was overgrown, roof shingles were missing. Celeste piped up crossly, "This ain't no school. It just be an empty house."

Mary Bethune laughed. "You see only a rented house. But when I look at this house, I see the future! Now, let's have some introductions." A small boy was pressed against her side. "This is my son, Albert. He's just four and the only boy allowed in our school. Your classmates are"—she indicated each girl in turn—"Anne, Lucille, Ruth, Lena, and Celeste."

Celeste recognized Lena from the shanty next door to theirs. She relaxed her scowl slightly. Maybe school wouldn't be so bad if Lena was there, Celeste thought.

Mrs. Bethune threw the door open wide. “Girls,” she announced, almost reverently, “enter these doors to learn and depart to serve.”

The little group of girls and mothers walked silently into the house and looked around. There were four large rooms on the first floor, with real glass windows. A narrow staircase disappeared to three small rooms upstairs. In spite of the repair work needed on the house outside, inside the house had been swept clean and the windows washed. A packing box had been set in place as the teacher’s desk.

“Classrooms downstairs, sleeping rooms upstairs,” said Mrs. Bethune. “The back room on the left will be the kitchen—when we can find a cookstove. Now, shall we get started with the opening of our first school day?”

Mary Bethune led the little group in singing “Leaning on the Everlasting Arms,” and then they recited the Twenty-third Psalm. Celeste listened in rapt attention to Mrs. Bethune’s rich, low voice and wondered why tears were sliding down her mother’s face.

Then Mrs. Bethune opened a big black book with gold-edged pages. “Listen,” she said. “From the gospel of John, chapter three, verse sixteen: ‘For God so loved the world, that he gave his only begotten Son, that whosoever believeth in him should not perish, but have everlasting life.’

“Did you hear that word ‘whosoever’?” she asked. Her warm, steady eyes looked at each girl in turn. “God said ‘whosoever’! That means you, Anne, and you, Lucille, and Ruth and Lena and Celeste and Albert. He didn't say just white folks. He didn't say just rich folks. He said 'whosoever' believes would have everlasting life."

Mary Bethune's chin went up. "That's where your dignity comes from—from that 'whosoever.' It's God who gives it to you! It's God who created you, who sent His Son to die for you. That means 'whosoever' believes—rich or poor, black or white—will live together with God in heaven."

There was a moment of silence as she let this sink in, a silence broken when Celeste demanded, "Do the white folks know that?"

"Raise your hand before you speak," Mrs. Bethune scolded gently, but her mouth betrayed a smile. "Some do. Let me tell you a story. . . ." The girls leaned closer.

"One day not so many years ago, a Quaker lady in Colorado named Mary Crissman felt God wanted her to help a poor Negro girl get an education. She wrote to Scotia Seminary in Concord, North Carolina, and asked for the name of a girl 'who would make good.' Miss Wilson, my teacher in Mayesville, South Carolina, submitted my name for the scholarship. I had been praying night and day for a way to keep going to school. That's how I first learned about 'victory through faith.' Because Mary Crissman, a white woman, paid for my entire education at Scotia Seminary for the Daughters of Freedmen, as well as a year at Moody Bible Institute." She smiled broadly. "When I get to heaven, I'm going to thank Mary Crissman in person."

Celeste's hand shot up. "What be 'daughters of freedmen'?"

"Celeste, wait until I call on you," Mrs. Bethune scolded again. "And the correct English is: '*Who are* the daughters of freedmen?'" But she went on to answer the question. "A freedman is someone who used to be a slave but has been freed. My father and mother were born in slavery, but the Emancipation Proclamation freed them in 1863. I was born twelve years later—born *free*. So were you born free. But now we have to learn how to *live* free. That's what this school is all about."

When the mothers had finally gone home, it was time for "life lessons," as Mrs. Bethune called them. "Just be same thing as chores," Celeste muttered to herself as they pumped water from the sulphur well, scrubbed the floors, took down the yellowed curtains at the windows, and hemmed up fresh muslin for new curtains. Celeste didn't like sewing; she kept poking her finger with the needle. But it was fun pulling Spanish moss off the big oak trees to stuff into mattress covers to sleep on. They made a campfire to heat up their supper of beans, and they poked sweet potatoes into the coals to bake. When the fire was cool, Mary Bethune showed the girls how to carefully pry off splinters from the charred wood. "Our pencils!" she said proudly.

Before evening prayers, Mrs. Bethune handed out five new toothbrushes and baking soda. Celeste's eyes widened. She had never owned her own toothbrush before. But the baking soda made her mouth pucker.

When the girls finally lay down on their moss-filled mattresses, Celeste realized she hadn't "played" all day.

✧ ✧ ✧ ✧

"Celeste, come along. It's your turn to be my assistant for our errands today," said Mary Bethune briskly.

Celeste jumped up guiltily. She was supposed to be practicing her letters with a pile of charcoal-splinter "pencils," but she had thrown them angrily off the back porch when she kept getting the J, K, and L backwards. She was only too glad to wash her hands at the kitchen pump and scurry after Mary Bethune.

Being Mrs. Bethune's assistant usually meant knocking door-to-door in various neighborhoods—white and black alike—telling about the school and listing the school's needs. "Excuse me, ma'am," she would say politely when the lady of the house would come to the door. "Have you heard about the Daytona Educational and Industrial School for Negro Girls?"

Sometimes they were met with a bored stare or a suspicious "Well?"

But Mrs. Bethune seemed not to notice, and with a happy smile she eagerly explained that this was a new kind of school. "We are training girls in head, hand, and heart," she'd say. "Their heads to think, their hands to work, their hearts to have faith."

By the time she was done, many people made a small donation or offered contributions of old furniture, a set of dishes, a sack of flour, stew vegetables, soup bones, needles and thread, material or hand-me-down clothing, even an old sewing machine.

"Someday we will have uniforms," promised Mrs. Bethune, lengthening a dress for one of the older girls. "Blue for every day and white for Sundays. But until then we must thank God for the clothes that cover our backs now."

Mornings were for book lessons. Their textbooks were a blue-black speller ("given to me by my first teacher when I was eleven years old," she explained fondly), *Maury's Geography*, a leather-bound book of poems by John Greenleaf Whittier, an old arithmetic book, and the *Fisk Jubilee Songbook*.

But in the afternoons she put the girls to work fixing up the school. They picked elderberries and boiled down the juice for ink. They combed the town dump and brought home anything that might be useful: a dented pot was pounded back into usefulness, thrown-out milking stools became chairs, old rugs were beaten to get rid of the dust and dirt and covered the bare floors. It was like a game, and each evening they all bragged about their latest "finds."

This particular afternoon Celeste tried to keep up with Mary Bethune's long strides as they headed up the path to a farmhouse where a gentle black-and-white cow sleepily chewed its cud in the shade of a large oak. Bypassing the front door, the woman and girl went around to the back and knocked.

The door was opened by a white woman with untidy gray hair, wearing a dirty apron. "Yep, I've heard of your school," she said, not unpleasantly, when Mary explained her mission. "Frankly, I'm just as glad someone's living in that abandoned house up the way," she said. "Surprised you're using it for a school, though. 'Spose you'll be stopping at third grade—that's as far as the colored can learn, my pastor says."

Celeste felt Mrs. Bethune stiffen beside her, but the teacher only cleared her throat and said mildly, "I see you've got a cow. Would you have any milk to spare for the children? We don't have money to pay you, but—"

"Why, funny you should ask," said the woman. "I churn butter to sell—helps make ends meet. But I have more buttermilk than I know what to do with. Just have to throw it out." She looked Mary Bethune up and down. "You seem like a right nice colored woman—know your place and all, coming to the back door proper-like. You just bring your own bucket, and you can take away as much buttermilk as you like."

Mrs. Bethune's smile was genuine. "Thank you very much," she beamed. "God will bless you for it."

"Say," said the woman as they started to turn away, "there is something you could do for me. I 'spose you can read, since you're teaching school and all. I've got this letter from my son up in Chicago, but—silly me—I've misplaced my spectacles somewhere. Could you read it to me?"

"Why, of course," said Mrs. Bethune graciously. They followed the woman into the worn kitchen as she fished in her apron pocket for the letter.

Just then Celeste spied the woman's spectacles lying on the table. "Why, there's your—OW!" she cut off her sentence with a howl. Mary Bethune had just stepped on her bare toes, hard.

The letter was read, thanks were again exchanged, and they were back on the path down to the road when Celeste said angrily, "Why you be so nice to that white-trash woman? Huh! She be puttin' on airs pretending she can read—and you been to college!"

"Hush now, Celeste," said Mrs. Bethune sternly. "I understand your feelings, but what good would it do to make her our enemy? The Good Book says, 'A soft answer turneth away wrath.' And the great Mr. Lincoln said about the defeated Southerners at the close of the Civil War: 'We destroy our enemies when we make them our friends.'"

Just then a voice called after them from the farmhouse door. "You all might just as well come get that old cookstove that's out behind the cow shed. Ain't doing me no good."

A smile spread broadly over Mary Bethune's face as she waved her thanks. "Victory through faith!" she said to Celeste and marched triumphantly down the road.

Chapter 5

Sweet Potato Peels

NEARLY EVERY WEEK one or two more girls were brought to the school by eager parents, until by spring of 1905 there were forty girls, and the little school was filled to bursting. In nice weather they had their lessons outside in the shade of the big oaks that filled the property. A second house was rented for a dormitory. On Sundays the girls were scrubbed and combed and braided and marched to church. Church lasted far too long for Celeste's liking—sometimes two or three hours of sitting on hard benches!—but she liked the singing.

Rise, shine, give God
the glory!
In the year of jubilee!

Oh, how the people clapped and cried and filled the little wooden church with song.

And then Mr. Albertus Bethune arrived. Little Albert was thrilled to see his daddy, and Mary Bethune seemed to smile more than usual. She eagerly showed her husband what they had accomplished so far at Daytona Educational and Industrial School: four reading group levels using a stack of donated readers, Bible memory, Latin grammar, Greek classics and American literature (read to the girls by Mrs. Bethune), arithmetic and simple algebra, and world geography. She had developed a simple uniform for the girls—blue dresses with white pinafores—and in the afternoon the girls were kept busy with sewing, cooking, weeding the school garden, washing, and ironing.

"He sure be one handsome-lookin' man," Lena whispered to Celeste one day as the two girls sat on the back porch of the schoolhouse, peeling sweet potatoes for Mrs. Bethune's latest money-raising project: baking and selling sweet potato pies. "An' he dress good, too." Mr. Bethune had his tailored sleeves rolled up and was chopping wood for the cookstove while little Albert gleefully gathered up the flying chips for kindling.

"Got one sweet-as-honey voice, too," murmured Celeste, remembering Mr. Bethune's rich tenor blending with his wife's alto at church the previous Sunday. "That man can sing—ow!" she yelped, dropping the peeling knife and grabbing her thumb. "Ow—ow—ow, I'm cut!" she wailed.

Mrs. Bethune appeared at the back door, sleeves rolled up, flour dusted on her apron. "Let me see, Celeste," she said calmly. "Just a nick—come on, we'll wash it and put on a bandage."

"You think of more ways ta get out of peelin' potatoes, Celeste Key," Lena muttered. "Yesterday it was a stomachache, and the day before . . ."

Pots of sweet potatoes were boiling on the cookstove, and the smell of fresh pies filled the kitchen. Some of the older girls were rolling out dough and seasoning sweet potato mash with cinnamon and cloves. *Why do I get stuck peelin' the dumb potatoes while the older girls have all the fun?* Celeste grumbled to herself, as her thumb was neatly wrapped with a clean rag.

"Now go clean up those peels," said Mrs. Bethune. "Always finish a job; don't leave the cleanup for someone else. Besides, stray peelings could cause an accident if someone slipped and fell. Oh, thank you, Albertus!" Mary Bethune came out on the porch, where her husband and son were filling the woodbox. "It sure is nice to have a man about," she beamed.

Mr. Bethune rolled down his sleeves but didn't smile. "That's what I want to talk to you about, Mary," he said. "Could we—?"

The husband and wife walked around the side of the house. Celeste could hear the rise and fall of their voices but couldn't make out what they were saying. She quickly scooped up the stray peelings into a pail and hurried to the compost pile, which lay just on the edge of the vegetable garden along the side of the house. From here Celeste could hear clearly, but the Bethunes did not seem to notice her.

"This is ridiculous, Mary," Albertus Bethune was saying. "Selling pies to support the school! Why, you and the girls are living hand-to-mouth, day-to-day. You don't even have a salary! Look at you—still wearing the same dress you were wearing the day you left Palatka. I want better than that for you and Albert."

"I know you do, Albertus," said his wife. "You mean well... but I don't want or need fancy clothes or fine furniture. I want *this*—forty girls learning how to read, how to speak properly, how to learn skills that will carry them far in life. And more girls are coming every day. The need is so great!"

"Exactly," the man said in frustration. "Forty girls, and you're trying to do everything yourself. It can't be done! You'll soon wear yourself out. Mary, please come back with me to Palatka. We both had teaching jobs there, a salary from the school district, a comfortable life... why can't you be happy there?"

There was a long pause. "Because it wasn't my school," said Mrs. Bethune finally. "That school district didn't expect much—why, 'they're only colored children, after all.' Oh, Albertus, you know my dream! A school like Scotia Seminary, with beautiful buildings and grounds, a place of dignity and learning, filled with music and art and literature... and more. I want to train doctors and nurses and college professors and engineers and chemists."

Mr. Bethune gave a short laugh and gestured

around him at the scruffy-looking house. "With *this*? By selling pies to railroad gangs and rich tourists?"

Mrs. Bethune lifted her chin. "A person has to start somewhere. A dream doesn't happen overnight." She laid a hand on her husband's arm. "Oh, Albertus, stay here with me. You could help teach! There's so much to do. We could work on the dream together!"

"Someone in this family needs to earn a living," he said curtly.

"Well, then, get a job in Daytona. Surely an educated man like you—"

"I've been looking, Mary. The only thing I've found is driving a horse-drawn taxi. No... I'm going back to my old teaching job in Palatka. It's a sure thing—not like this wild scheme of yours. And if you'd come to your senses, I'm sure you could get your old job back, too."

Celeste was standing openmouthed as she eavesdropped on the handsome couple—until she realized Mary Bethune had looked up, caught her eye, and frowned. Quickly, Celeste grabbed her pail and ran back to the house. But as she scurried around the corner, she heard Mrs. Bethune say, "I'll write you, Albertus... every week."

✧ ✧ ✧ ✧

"My stomach hurts, Mrs. Keyser," Celeste complained, looking up mournfully at the new teacher. Mrs. Bethune had hired the young black teacher from New York, promising her $3.50 a week plus room and board. Widowed shortly after her marriage, Frances Keyser had answered Mrs. Bethune's ad in the hopes of leaving her sorrow behind.

Lena rolled her eyes. "Girl, you just tired of peeling sweet potatoes. Look; everyone done but you 'cause you slow as molasses."

By the fall of 1905, the pie-baking business was thriving. Sweet potatoes were cheap and plentiful. Many of the railroad workers were single men living in bunkhouses in the shanty town, only too willing to fork over fifteen cents of their wages for a home-baked pie. The pies were popular with rich tourists, as well. Contributing to a "vocational training school" for Negro children in the South was an acceptable charity for northern whites, and the pies were "a charming southern treat."

But peeling sweet potatoes was dreary work, and Celeste kept inventing new ways to get out of the disagreeable chore. Mrs. Keyser was new; maybe the stomachache would work with her.

Just then Mrs. Bethune stuck her head out of the door. "Remember our Bible reading this morning, Celeste?" she asked cheerfully. "'Whatsoever ye do in word or deed, do all in the name of the Lord Jesus!' I'm sure the apostle Paul would include peeling potatoes."

Mrs. Bethune went back inside, but her voice floated through the screen door. "Let's sing, girls!" she urged. "That's how we made the days go fast when I was a girl picking cotton in Georgia. Come on, now... the good, old spirituals." And she launched into *"Nobody knows the trouble I've seen..."*

Some of the girls baking pies laughed good-naturedly and joined in. Mrs. Keyser picked it up, too, and soon the song was filling the air: *"...Nobody knows like Jesus."*

The last few notes of the old Negro spiritual had faded away, and Celeste was alone on the porch, attacking her last potato, when she heard a man clear his throat at the side of the house. “Celeste, that be you? I’ve come to take you home.”

Celeste jumped up, spilling her potato peels. “Papa!” she cried happily. She’d forgotten that it was Saturday and her turn to go home overnight. She ran inside the house to tell Mrs. Bethune that her papa had come and was just skipping out the front door to meet him at the front gate, when Mrs. Bethune called after them, “Mr. Key, one moment, please!”

The big man pulled his cap off his head and waited.

“Mr. Key, do you vote?” Mrs. Bethune asked.

He looked startled. Then a scornful smile creased his face. “Now, Mrs. Bethune, do I look like a man who votes? Just walk right up to the voting booth, easy as you please, nod goodday to the white man, and mark my ballot?”

“It’s your right as a citizen,” she said boldly.

His eyes narrowed. “Don’t mock me, lady. Colored man could get hisself lynched for less.” He grabbed Celeste’s hand and stalked off angrily. “That woman gonna get us all in a heap o’ trouble with her big ideas,” he said under his breath.

Celeste ignored his muttering. She was used to her papa’s grumbling when it came to Mrs. Bethune and the school. But she had a surprise for this visit home she was sure even her papa would like.

Baby Button was almost two and walking now. He squealed with delight when Samuel and Celeste came up the shanty path. Mama wanted to hear all the latest news from the school; even Tom and Buddy listened with interest as she chatted away. And the corn bread from Mama's secondhand cookstove was melt-in-her-mouth good.

"Now, Mama... Papa, I've got a surprise," said Celeste, jumping up from the table and taking down the old family Bible from its shelf. The Bible had been handed down from Lilly's parents, but as far as Celeste knew, no one in her family could read it.

The little shanty seemed to hold its breath as Celeste turned the pages of the old Bible. Then she began to read: "Psalm 23... 'The Lord is my shepherd; I shall not want....'"

When she had read the entire psalm, Celeste looked up. Tears glistened on her mother's cheeks. "Ain't that somethin'," whispered Mama, all choked up. "Nine years old and readin' straight from the Bible itself." Samuel Key didn't say anything, but, as Celeste suspected, he looked proud as a peacock.

Only Lucy was stonefaced. "You think you somethin' high 'n mighty, just 'cause you can read and talk all proper-like," she hissed to Celeste as the girls got ready for bed. "Just remember who does all the real work 'round here. At least I be good for somethin'."

"Huh, you're just jealous 'cause you can't read," snorted Celeste. "Probably too old and too dumb to read. Why, you ain't no different than Willy the mule. He's a good worker, too—*ow*! Mama!" she screeched. "Lucy pulled my hair!"

Except for the sullen glares from Lucy all day Sunday, Celeste enjoyed her weekend visit. But she skipped happily up to the front door of the school when it was time to return. After one year, school had become "home," too.

But when Celeste entered the schoolroom, something seemed wrong. Girls were cooking supper in the kitchen, but instead of laughing and talking, there were only hushed whispers. Two girls came out of the back room, their eyes puffy from crying. Several more looked at Celeste, then walked away.

Just then Frances Keyser came out of the back room, pulling the door shut gently, her pretty young face lined with worry.

"Mrs. Keyser!" Celeste cried. "What's wrong? Has something happened?"

Mrs. Keyser nodded, troubled. "Yes, something's happened... Mrs. Bethune has had an accident. We think—we don't know—that her arm is broken."

Other girls gathered around and began chattering nervously. "We ran got a neighbor, and he took her to the hospital in his wagon."

"But the doctor said they don't admit colored folks in a white hospital!"

"So the neighbor had to turn around and bring her back!"

"Can you believe that? Wouldn't let Mrs. Bethune in their stinking old hospital!"

Celeste's head was spinning. "But... but what happened? How—?"

Lena leaned close to Celeste's ear and hissed, "She fell down the back porch steps. *Somebody* forgot to clean up her potato peels."

Chapter 6

All Men Are Created Equal

CELESTE FELT TERRIBLE. She wanted to run right out the door and find someplace to hide... but Frances Keyser gave her a nudge. "Go on—go see her." With heavy steps Celeste walked over to the door of the back room and knocked timidly.

"Come in," said a faint voice.

Celeste stepped into the dim room. Mrs. Bethune was propped up on a narrow bed with her arm, all wrapped in bandages, resting at her side on the top of the blankets. Pain dulled her normally bright eyes. But she said warmly, "Come here, child."

Celeste hung her head. "I didn't mean to leave the peelings on the back steps, Mrs. Bethune," she said miserably. "B-but Papa came, an' I forgot—" She burst into tears.

"Hush, now," soothed Mrs. Bethune. "I know you didn't mean to. But the fact is, the things we do and say have consequences, whether we mean them or not. Isn't that true?"

Celeste sniffed and nodded. Then she had a horrible thought. "Are... are you gonna kick me outta the school?"

A smile tipped the corners of Mrs. Bethune's mouth. "Of course not. But since I'm laid up here, I think you can keep me company and recite your lessons to me tomorrow. You've been lagging behind... getting lazy in your work. Tomorrow can be your catch-up day, all right?"

The next morning, Celeste tried to look repentant (was she being punished? she wondered), but it was hard not to gloat to Lena and the other girls about keeping Mrs. Bethune company all by herself for the whole morning. But, oh, how she worked! Sitting on the teacher's bed, she conjugated verbs, struggled through the capitals of all forty-six states, and recited the multiplication tables. But halfway through a list of new spelling words, Celeste grumbled, "Why do I have to learn how to spell words like 'democratic'? It don't have nothin'—I mean, doesn't have anything—to do with me, anyhow."

Mrs. Bethune settled back against the pillows with a sigh and gazed at a picture of her parents on a little bedside table. Then she said, "Let me tell you a story, Celeste."

Celeste gladly let the spelling book slip to the floor.

"My mother took in washing for white folks, just like your mother does, at the same plantation where she used to be a slave. One day when I was about five years old, I went with her to the Wilson place to take back some laundry. I liked to go there because the Wilson girls had a lot of toys, and sometimes we played together. On this particular day, I saw a children's book and picked it up. 'Show me an A,' I demanded eagerly. But the book was snatched out of my hands. 'You can't read,' said one of my little white friends. 'You're black.'"

Celeste blinked guiltily. Did Mrs. Bethune know how she'd taunted her sister Lucy just two days earlier? No, that was impossible! On the other hand, from the very first day she'd met this self-assured, determined woman, it felt as if she could read her thoughts and see into her soul.

But Mrs. Bethune continued, the emotions of that long-ago day as fresh as this morning's dew. "I ran home in tears. *Why can white children read but not black children?* I wondered. My parents had always told me I was the first child of theirs to be born free—but I wondered what 'free' meant. White people had fine clothes and respect and all kinds of jobs. But it seemed that the only thing black people had was hard work and each other. Maybe, I thought, maybe the difference was that white people could read."

Mrs. Bethune looked meaningfully at Celeste, even as she winced with pain when she moved. "That very day I promised myself that someday I would learn to read. And when I learned how to read, I

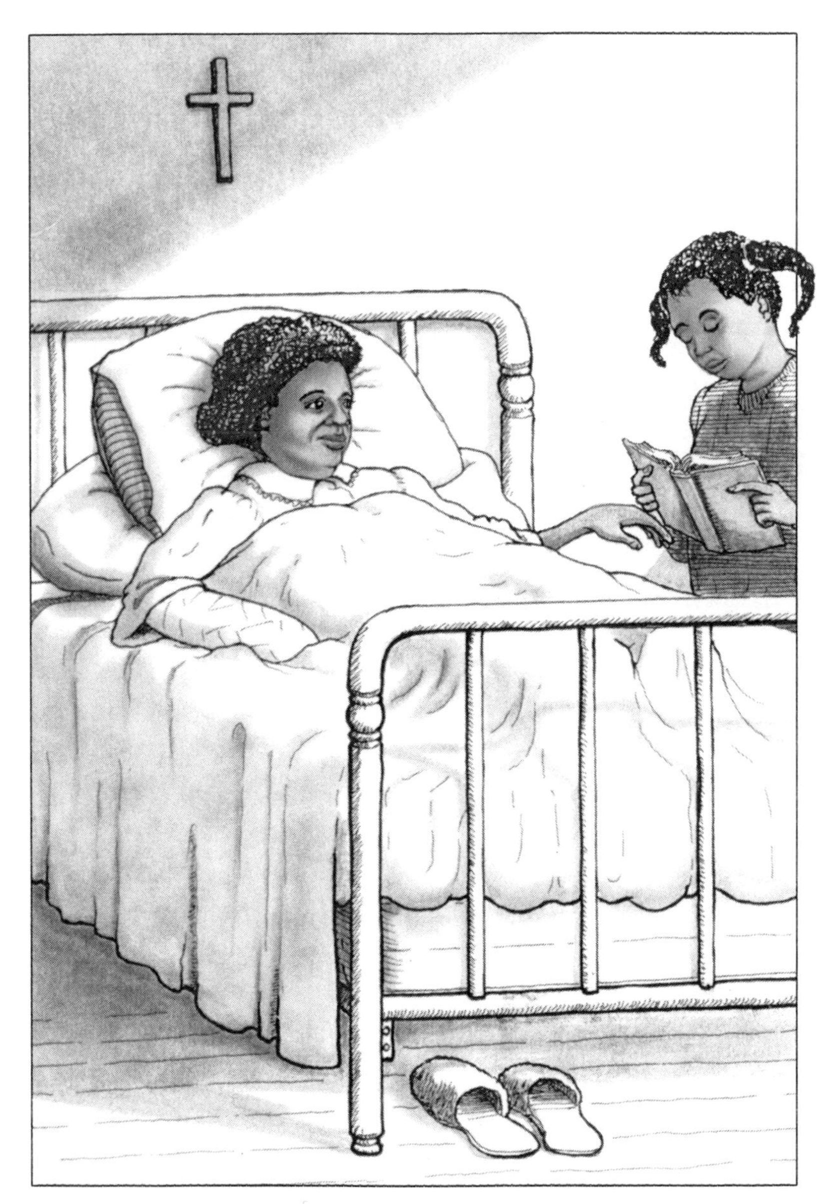

decided my goal in life was to help every man, woman, and child learn how to read, also. It's the key that unlocks all the other doors in life, Celeste—starting with the Bible and including the Declaration of Independence, which says, 'We hold these truths to be self-evident, that all men are created equal....' That," she said, pointing at the spelling book on the floor, "is why you need to learn how to spell words like 'democratic'!"

Without a word, Celeste obediently picked up the book. She felt ashamed for having taunted her sister about not being able to read. Maybe . . . For the first time in her life, Celeste thought about what she might want to do when she was a grown woman. Maybe she could be a teacher like Mrs. Bethune and help people learn to read! And just as quickly, the thought died. Mrs. Bethune was good and kind and wise. Celeste didn't feel like she was good; hadn't her parents told her a hundred times that she was lazy and no-good? As for kind and wise—

A loud knock on the front door of the school interrupted her thoughts. "Oh, dear, you'll have to get it, Celeste," said Mrs. Bethune, sinking back onto the pillows. "Mrs. Keyser and the girls are outside having lessons. Just tell the person to come back later. I-I don't have the energy to deal with guests."

The knocking persisted. Smoothing her dress and pinafore, Celeste left the bedroom and opened the front door a crack. An unfamiliar black man in top hat and graying hair, black coat, and starched white collar stood at the door. A horse-drawn taxi waited at the gate.

"May I speak to Mrs. Mary McLeod Bethune, please?" he said with a polite little bow.

Celeste opened the door a few more inches. "Come back later, please. Mrs. Bethune ain't—I mean, Mrs. Bethune can't see you right now. She's had an accident."

"An accident?" The man looked alarmed. "What do you mean? Is she—? Miss, you must let me in!" He pushed against the door, but, frightened, Celeste slammed the door shut and was just about to slide the lock when she heard Frances Keyser's voice behind her.

"Celeste? Who is at the door?" The young teacher reopened the door, and there stood a very distraught gentleman.

"Mrs. Bethune?" he said.

"No, I'm her assistant."

"Oh!" he said, somewhat surprised. "Well, Ma'am, my name is Dr. Madison Mason, head of the Methodist Episcopal Fund for Southern Education. I was on my yearly tour to inspect our mission schools when I heard about the school Mrs. Bethune had started here in Daytona. I have made a special trip to become acquainted with Mrs. Bethune and her school, but I understand—"

"Oh, please, sir, do come in," said Mrs. Keyser, flustered. "Celeste, run put on the tea water."

When Celeste brought back a pot of tea, turning the cracked side away from the guest, Dr. Mason was saying, "The hospital turned her away? She hasn't been seen by a doctor?" The muscles in the man's face tightened angrily. "This is outrageous! She must have medical attention immediately or the injury may become permanent. Please, let me see her."

The tea was forgotten as Dr. Mason, Mrs. Keyser, and Mrs. Bethune consulted behind the closed door. The schoolgirls, temporarily forgotten, did their noon-time chores, made excuses to come into the house and look at the closed door, asked Celeste a hundred times who the man was and what he looked like, and somehow managed to eat their lunch of bread, black-eyed peas, and fresh buttermilk.

When the back room door finally opened, the man strode to the front door and called to the man waiting in the taxi. Within a few minutes, the two men and Mrs. Keyser were carefully helping Mrs. Bethune into the taxi and handing her a bag with some of her clothes. The girls crowded on the porch and in the yard, watching wide-eyed.

As the taxi drove off, the girls peppered Mrs. Keyser with questions all at once. "Girls! Girls!" she said desperately, trying to calm them. But she looked as worried as they did. "Dr. Mason has convinced Mrs. Bethune to let him take her home with him to Chicago—"

"Chicago!" gasped forty voices at once.

"—to be seen by his personal doctor. She needs weeks of rest and care."

"But what are we going to do?" wailed several

girls. "We can't have school without Mrs. Bethune!"

Frances Keyser swallowed hard and then lifted her chin. "Yes, we can, because *Mrs. Bethune* thinks we can. Now—what does Mrs. Bethune say to do when the task before you is hard?"

Celeste suddenly grinned. "Sing!" she shouted. Some of the other girls giggled nervously.

"Exactly," said the young teacher. "We're going to sing. We're going to learn parts. We're going to have a choir. We're going to work hard and surprise Mrs. Bethune when she returns." She looked around, challenging the girls with the spark in her eyes. "Are you game? Are we going to work together?"

Her last words were lost in the cheer that threatened to shake the loose shingles from the roof of the little schoolhouse on Oak Street.

✧ ✧ ✧ ✧

"Here she comes!" squealed the lookout at the window, scurrying back to her place facing the front door. Weeks had passed, but finally word had arrived that Mary Bethune was coming home from Chicago. The girls were nervous and excited. Informal singing had always been a part of their daily routine at the school, but Frances Keyser had taught them a new hymn by a black songwriter named Charles Tindley, one she'd learned in New York.

Through the curtained windows, Celeste could see Mrs. Bethune paying the horse-drawn taxi driver, then come walking up the path to the porch. Celeste licked her dry lips. As the door opened, Mrs. Keyser gave the signal, and forty voices opened their mouths in harmony singing a hymn by Charles Tindley.

When the storms of life are raging,
Stand by me;
When the storms of life are raging,
Stand by me;
When the world is tossing me,
Like a ship upon the sea;
Thou who rulest wind and water,
Stand by me.

Mrs. Bethune stood in the doorway, transfixed, as the girls sang all five verses of the hymn. Tears were in her eyes as the last note died away.

"Beautiful... absolutely beautiful," she breathed. "The most wonderful welcome home any teacher ever had." She turned to Frances Keyser and smiled broadly. "Mrs. Keyser, I think we have a choir on our hands."

At that, all the girls broke loose with a barrage of questions. "How is your arm?" "What is Chicago like?" "Was it cold?" She had come home as soon as the cast came off, Mrs. Bethune said, and the arm would be good as new. Chicago was an exciting place, but she was glad to be back home.

Only Celeste stood slightly apart, still hearing the music in her ears. Something had happened in the weeks Mrs. Bethune had been gone. She had discovered that she liked to sing. Instead of singing just to get through a disagreeable chore, she had started to enjoy singing for its own sake. Mrs. Keyser had taught her and some of the other girls to sing the second part, and she still felt awed at the wonder of singing harmony. They had worked hard to surprise Mrs. Bethune, but even as the girls eagerly welcomed back their teacher, Celeste felt a little sad. Was it over? Would they get a chance to sing like that again?

She should have known better. Mrs. Bethune never wasted anything, and she certainly wasn't going to waste an opportunity to show off what her girls could do in order to attract interested people, from parents to contributors. "Girls," she said, beaming, the very next day, "you're going to sing at church on Sunday! It's all arranged."

Word had gotten around, and the Mount Bethel Baptist Church was packed. To Celeste's astonishment, she saw her mother and father sitting among the people on the hard benches. Her father looked uncomfortable in a starched shirt, but her mother's face was beaming. It was the first time Celeste had seen either one of them in church.

The girls choir sang the Charles Tindley hymn, then followed with the traditional spiritual, "Sometimes I feel like a motherless chile." The congregation loved it and sang right along. After the sermon, the preacher asked the girls to come up and sing "Stand By Me" one more time. The "Amens!" and "Hallelujahs!" were almost deafening.

Lilly Key found Celeste after the service was over

and gave her a big hug. She was so proud. Samuel Key patted Celeste's shoulder. In his wordless way, she knew he was pleased, too.

Mrs. Bethune was shaking hands all around and introducing her newest teacher, Frances Keyser. When she got to the Keys, Mrs. Bethune pumped Samuel Key's hand and said, "Mr. Key, we're starting an evening civics class for adults at Daytona Educational and Industrial Institute soon. I'd be proud to enroll you in our class."

"Civics?" jumped in Lilly Key. "What be that?"

"Learning about your rights as a citizen—and your responsibilities," said Mrs. Bethune. "The Declaration of Independence, the Bill of Rights, the Constitution of the United States... they all belong to you, too."

"Huh!" snorted Smauel Key as he pulled Lilly away. "Ain't you heard that they're starting to lay off railroad workers? You think some useless class at your school goin' to get us decent jobs? You still under some delusion that white folks gonna let black folks be equal here in the South. Well, it ain't gonna happen. Not in my lifetime! You just wastin' your time."

Chapter 7

Greek and a Toothbrush

"But, Papa!" Celeste argued. "Other railroad men are coming to the evening classes. Why, just the other day I heard that Lena's papa got himself registered to vote. He took the test at city hall and paid the dollar-fifty tax, too. The white folks couldn't do a thing about it, either; they had to let him register."

Celeste's second year at Mrs. Bethune's school was moving swiftly, and things seemed to be changing every day. Word spread quickly about the Negro girls choir, and suddenly there were invitations from all over Daytona to come sing—from black churches, white churches, civic groups, even at some of the tourist hotels. Mrs. Bethune accepted them all. Exposure meant goodwill, and

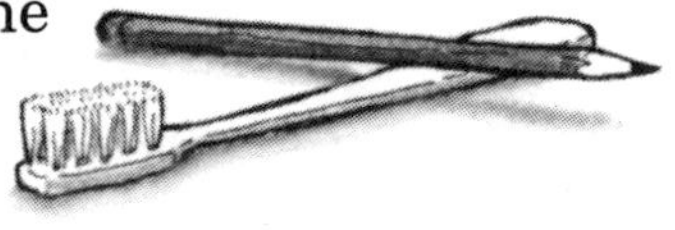

goodwill meant new students and contributors and patrons of the school.

As a result, many new girls enrolled throughout 1906, until Celeste lost count of how many. Mrs. Bethune hired several new teachers and rented another house nearby for dormitory space and classrooms. The "night school" for adults boasted a homemaking class in addition to the civics class, and on her visits home, Celeste talked up the classes, hoping her parents would participate.

"True enough?" Samuel Key seemed surprised when he heard about Lena's daddy. Then he shook his head suspiciously. "Registerin' be one thing; we'll see whether they'll let him vote come the next election," he said, wagging his finger.

"Life training"—making and selling pies, hoeing the school's vegetable garden, sewing their own clothes—was still plain old hard work to Celeste, and even though she was ten years old, she sometimes thought she would never master algebra and Latin verbs. But singing in the choir... *that* was different. The spirituals, hymns, and gospel songs grew deep in her heart. All the attention from blacks and whites alike wasn't bad, either. So, since staying in school was the only way to sing in the choir, Celeste studied.

Singing at the luxurious Palmetto Hotel was like stepping into another world for Celeste and the other girls. Crystal chandeliers sparkled in the lobby. Plush carpet ran alongside polished marble floors. The lady guests wore silk dresses and fancy hats with feathers,

and the men wore tailored suits, top hats, and carried walking canes. A Negro doorman held open the front door for them, and another uniformed bellhop showed them to the hotel ballroom.

They had been invited to sing at a special tea at

the hotel. As they lined up in rows, wearing their Sunday uniforms of white dresses and white stockings with white ribbons in their hair, Celeste heard murmurs of "How sweet!" and "Aren't they darling?"

And then they sang. As the music of the old spirituals and hymns filled the ballroom, the rustling and murmuring stopped and people listened. Afterward, Celeste even saw a few ladies dabbing at their eyes with their lace handkerchiefs.

An older gentleman in a pinstriped suit with a white handkerchief tucked neatly in his breast pocket made his way to Mrs. Bethune. "You are doing a wonderful work, madame," he said, taking her hand and shaking it warmly. "I have never seen anything like it. Tell me more about your school."

Mrs. Bethune never needed much of an invitation to talk about her school. As the other teachers rounded up the girls to walk home, she was heard saying, "I need a board, Mr. Gamble—trustees, fund-raisers. I need men like you. Will you come to the school and see for yourself?"

The girls were busy at their lessons a week later, when Celeste looked out the window and saw one of those newfangled motorcars stop in front of the schoolhouse. A man in a pinstriped suit stepped out and was greeted warmly by Mrs. Bethune on the front path.

Curious students and teachers alike crowded at the open windows of the classrooms. No white man had ever visited the Daytona Educational and Industrial Institute before. And this was no ordinary white man. He was obviously *very* rich.

"And where is this wonderful school you have been telling me about, Mrs. Bethune?" the man said, looking about curiously as if he might be in the wrong place. "You said something about a main building called Faith Hall—"

Celeste and the other girls looked at one another in dismay. Mrs. Bethune had a way of talking about her dreams for the school as if they were already a reality: brick buildings, science labs, a landscaped campus. But suddenly the girls saw the school as the man must be seeing it: a shabby little house with missing shingles on a dirt street at the north end of Shanty Town.

Then Mrs. Bethune's strong, rich voice floated to them through the open windows. "It's in my heart, Mr. Gamble!" she said. "All that I described to you at the hotel will someday be a reality. But we need money, Mr. Gamble—money and support from the wider community."

The man looked at her with a mixture of disbelief and admiration. "I understand there is currently a debate between what kind of education is best for Negro children, Mrs. Bethune. Booker T. Washington makes an excellent argument for a practical education, giving them skills at trades that will support their families and make them useful citizens—like his own Tuskegee Institute. And then there is W. E. B. DuBois, who insists that the Negro as well as the white should receive a classical education, including Greek and literature." He tilted his head curiously. "What do you think, Mrs. Bethune?"

The sturdy woman looked back at him with unflinching eyes. "*Both*, Mr. Gamble. Greek *and* a toothbrush—that's my philosophy! My school seeks to educate the head, the hand, and the heart."

Mr. Gamble threw back his head and laughed aloud. "I like your spirit, Mrs. Bethune." He withdrew a slim checkbook from the inside of his coat. "I am happy to donate to your school, and I will be honored to become its very first trustee."

The whole school was abuzz about this exciting turn of events. Over the next few weeks, Mr. Gamble—who had made his fortune manufacturing soap—showed up with a parade of potential trustees to talk to Mrs. Bethune about her vision for the school. One man, smartly dressed, went from classroom to classroom, observing the girls at work. He seemed especially interested in the sewing room. Lena was in the room at the time and told Celeste about it later. "You know that old, rusty sewing machine we have? Well, that man marched up to it, glared at the lettering, and muttered, 'Singer, eh?'—then just marched out again. Why in the world do you think he was interested in that broken-down old thing? I can barely push the treadle."

The next day a delivery wagon pulled up in front of the school. When the boxes were unpacked, there were three brand-new sewing machines with the name "WHITE" painted on each one in swirling gold letters. Mrs. Bethune laughed out loud. "That was Mr. White, who owns the White Sewing Machine

Company," she chuckled. "He just sent me a note saying he is joining our board of trustees."

✧ ✧ ✧ ✧

Soon Mrs. Bethune's school had its board of trustees, including Rev. A. L. James of Mount Bethel Baptist Church, Daytona's largest Negro congregation, and several wealthy whites. But in spite of the school's goodwill, tension was building between blacks and local whites in Daytona. The middle leg of Flagler's railroad was almost complete; many blacks had already been laid off, and most of Daytona's local residents wished the railroad workers would just go back where they came from.

But Mrs. Bethune's training was firm: the students must be equally courteous to white and black alike, whether rich or poor, friendly or rude. Each person was to be treated with respect and dignity.

By the fall of 1906, the sweet potato pie business had become a staple to the Daytona tourists, and Celeste—beginning her third year of school—was now helping with the deliveries. She loved walking into town with Mrs. Bethune, gaping at the fancy dresses and hats in the shop windows, feeling proud when richly dressed tourists hailed Mrs. Bethune and said, "Aren't you the teacher with that wonderful girls choir? Oh! And is this one of your talented girls?"

One day as Mrs. Bethune, seven-year-old Albert, Celeste, and two of the older girls came out of a shop after delivering some pies, they passed a group of tourists. Albert raised his cap politely to the ladies, and the girls curtsied. Several of the ladies said, "Oh, how charming," and their male companions tipped their hats politely. But a few minutes later, as Mrs. Bethune mailed her weekly letter to Albertus, a local resident brushed past the little group without acknowledging the children's greeting.

Celeste looked after him crossly. "That man is so rude!" she said loudly. "He didn't even tip his hat to you, Mrs. Bethune."

Overhearing this comment, the man turned back, his puffy face red with anger. "How dare you speak to a city councilman like that! If you know what's good for you and your uppity Negro school, Mary," he said, jabbing a finger in her face, "you will teach these colored children to remember their place." With that he stalked off.

The children were upset, and even Mrs. Bethune walked home fast-paced and tight-lipped. "He called her by her first name—did it on purpose, too," said Celeste indignantly to the other girls.

"Can't speak to my mama like that," said little Albert stoutly. "I'm gonna punch him inna nose."

"Hush, Albert," said his mother. "Punching people in the nose never solved anything—what's this?"

She stopped abruptly. They had turned onto Oak Street, but several men were sitting around by the fence in front of the schoolhouse. They scrambled to their feet when they saw Mrs. Bethune and the children approaching and just stood there, silent, watching. One had a pitchfork; another a hammer. They looked big and rough.

"Let me do the talking, children," said Mrs. Bethune quietly, starting forward once more.

"But," said Celeste with sudden realization, "that's my daddy!"

Sure enough, Samuel Key stepped out of the little group. "What you need doin' round here, Mrs. Bethune?" he asked. "Coat of paint be one thing. And those shingles sure need tappin' down. Where you want us to start?"

Mrs. Bethune couldn't hide her surprise. "Why, the paint and shingles would be an excellent place to start," she said. "But—why this sudden offer of help, Mr. Key?"

"Can't come to your night class without payin' somethin'," he said sharply. "Hope some work round the place take care of my fee."

Celeste could hardly believe it. Her daddy was coming to night school! Without further ado, Samuel Key and his fellows put up a ladder and were soon swarming over the roof with hammers and nails.

Mrs. Bethune was smiling broadly as she and the children took their empty baskets inside. "And maybe down the road, Samuel Key," she murmured to herself, "you can help vote out a certain city councilman."

Chapter 8

Hell's Hole

AFTER NEARLY THREE YEARS at the Daytona Educational and Industrial Training School, Celeste had learned to recognize the determined look in Mrs. Bethune's eyes when she was up to something. And she was definitely up to something again.

At thirty-two years of age, Mrs. Bethune was in the prime of her life. Her sturdy body had thickened a bit about the waist, but her stride was still long, and she stayed up many nights working long after the girls and other teachers had gone to bed. This morning she had put on her hat, set Albert Jr. to work on his lessons, and disappeared down Oak Street on her

bicycle—riding west, away from town.

At lunchtime she reappeared just as Portia Smiley, one of the new teachers, had finished saying the blessing. "I have wonderful news!" Mrs. Bethune announced triumphantly. "I have just purchased a nice piece of property where we are going to build our new school!"

The girls broke out in excited chattering. "Where is it?" "Will it have a real dormitory?" "Can we each have our own bed?" New girls were continuing to enroll each term, but there were no more houses to rent on Oak Street, and "bunking up" had become the rule rather than the exception.

"Where did you say this property was?" asked Frances Keyser somewhat suspiciously. "And how much is it going to cost?"

"Oh, didn't I say?" said Mrs. Bethune, taking off her hat. "The man sold it to me for two hundred dollars, with only five dollars down. It's that large, empty lot on the north end of Shanty Town, along Second Avenue."

Josie Roberts, another new teacher, looked startled. "But, ma'am! That's the town dump!"

"And we don't *have* two hundred dollars," said Frances Keyser. She was Mrs. Bethune's right-hand woman and knew the school was running on a tight budget. "Fact is, how did you manage to scare up an extra five dollars?"

"Oh, dear," said Portia Smiley, genuinely worried. "I heard that dump was called 'Hell's Hole'—all sorts of riffraff hang out there."

"Ladies, ladies," said Mrs. Bethune. "You have to look beyond what *is* to what *will be*! The good Lord has brought us this far; He won't let us down now. Why, that property has beautiful towering oaks. I can see it now—a curving drive leading up to the main building, brick dormitories, a science building, our own chapel... why, all we have to do is get to work, cleaning up that dump, and..."

Which is exactly what they did. The entire school spent weeks during the summer of 1907 clearing out trash from Hell's Hole and cutting down overgrown weeds. Neighbors came by, shaking their heads at that crazy teacher-lady, then showed up with wagons and mules to help haul away everything from rusty metal bed frames and broken wagon wheels to tin cans and old shoes. The girls were put to work dragging burnable trash and scrub wood to a central spot and piling it high.

To Celeste's disgust, choir practice and invitations to sing were put on hold. There was simply too much work to do. But without choir practice and singing to look forward to, the hot summer days just seemed like one endless drudgery.

"This sure is Hell's Hole, all right. I thought slavery was outlawed in the last century," Celeste complained to Lena, as the two girls pulled at an old plow handle tangled among some dead brambles. The girls jumped as a scraggly yellow cat scurried out, yowling in protest. "Besides, this place gives me the creeps."

"Cats are better than rats," Lena said, wiping the sweat out of her eyes.

"Huh!" muttered Celeste. She hated the rats, too, but snakes were the worst. And she was glad when those tramps had moved on—the ones they'd found the first day of cleanup, sleeping on dirty, old mattresses in the dump and stinking of cheap whiskey. But Celeste still felt uneasy. Maybe they'd just moved on back into the woods surrounding the dump, full of slash pines, oaks, and hickory trees.

They'd been working on the dump for two weeks when Mrs. Bethune announced at suppertime, "Tonight we're going back to burn that big pile of trash—a bonfire party!"

There were shouts of "Hooray!" all around her, but Celeste groaned inwardly. That place was creepy enough in the daytime, but... *at night*?

"Mrs. Keyser," she said, sighing dramatically, "I think I'll stay home and go to bed. I don't feel too good."

Frances Keyser felt her forehead. "Hmm. You look fine to me, Celeste Key," she said calmly. "You might be eleven years old now, but we can't leave you here all by yourself. Come on; you'll enjoy it. It'll be like the Fourth of July!"

The bonfire leaped and sparked as dusk faded into nightfall. The girls got long twigs, stuck them in the fire, then danced about and "wrote in the air" with the burning embers. But Celeste hung back. There was something frightening about the huge fire, seeing the flames licking around the remains of people's furniture and old, wooden farm equipment. She looked away.

And then Celeste saw it. Something white, moving in the woods, just beyond the reach of the bonfire's glow. She shook her head and told herself she was seeing things in the dark—when she saw it again, just barely visible in the trees on the other side of the clearing.

Heart pounding, she stared anxiously into the darkness. What was it? *Who* was it? Then she saw them again—two... three... maybe four figures on horseback, all dressed in white robes. But they had no faces, only eyes.

Celeste tried to scream, but nothing came out. Scrambling through the dancing girls, she tugged on Mrs. Bethune's sleeve. "G-g-ghosts!" she gasped. "I saw ghost riders in the woods!" She pointed wildly to where the figures had been.

But nobody—or nothing—was there.

Mrs. Bethune put a comforting arm around her. "There is no such thing as ghosts, honey. That's superstitious talk."

"B-but, I saw something, Mrs. Bethune!" Celeste felt panic rising into her throat.

"Then maybe you saw some of those tramps who were living in the dump just trying to scare us," said the teacher soothingly. "Well, we won't be scared. Remember the words to that lovely hymn?... *I trust in God, I know He cares for me. On mountain bleak or on the stormy sea... My heavenly Father watches over me.*"

Mrs. Bethune let Celeste stay close beside her until the bonfire had burned itself out. But Celeste knew it wasn't tramps she'd seen. Tramps didn't wear white robes from head to toe. And tramps had faces, not just dark eyes.

That night in bed beside Lena, Celeste lay awake, still frightened. Mrs. Bethune said there wasn't any such thing as ghosts... but Celeste had seen something. And the more she thought about it, what she'd seen seemed vaguely familiar.

And then she remembered.

Statesboro. She'd seen figures dressed all in white robes like that in Statesboro, the night her papa's blacksmith shop got burned down.

✧ ✧ ✧ ✧

Celeste grunted as she and nine-year-old Buddy lifted the white sheets with sturdy sticks out of the hot, soapy washtub into the steaming rinse tub. Lucy was sick, and Celeste had been corralled into helping Mama and Buddy do the weekend laundry.

But her mind wasn't on the heavy, wet clothes. Should she tell her mama about what she'd seen in the woods around the new school property? Ever since the bonfire, she'd been having bad dreams about white-robed figures and burning torches. She desperately wanted to tell *somebody*—but Mama hadn't seen the mob that had burned down Papa's blacksmith shop. Would Mama know what she was talking about? Would it make her afraid?

Just then Samuel Key and Tom came strutting up the path, arms on each other's shoulders, singing loudly. *"I got a gal up Jackson way. Ain't got time ta get my pay—"*

"You hush, now, ya hear?" scolded Lilly Key, coming out of the shanty. "Don't you see children about? My, my, the things you two pick up from that Gandy Dancin' crew."

Somehow Papa and Tom had managed to hang on to jobs with Flagler's railroad, joining the select crew of "Gandy Dancers" who straightened the tracks when the rails got bent from the heavy weight of the trains.

"Gandy Dancers!" said Celeste. "What does that mean?"

"Dunno what it means," snorted Tom, "but we gotta work together in rhythm, all puttin' pressure on the rails on the same beat. Why, we be singin' an' clankin' our poles all day." He grinned. *"Look out, Sal, yore man be gone—"*

"Tom!" glared his mother. She came out to the rinse tub, muttering under her breath. "Why can't these railroad men sing the fine old spirituals and gospel hymns like Mrs. Bethune's choir? Don't know why they have ta mess up they minds with all them no-good drinkin' and flirtin' songs."

Tom just grinned and went inside to wash up. Samuel clucked Lilly playfully on the chin. "Now, Lilly, don't you go fussin'. Why, I'm learnin' to read, ain't I, at Mrs. Bethune's night school? Don't that make you happy?"

Lilly rolled her eyes and finally smiled reluctantly. "Go on, go on, wash up. We got work to do here.

Celeste, you feed the bedding into the ringer," Lilly directed. "Buddy, turn the crank. I'll do the hangin'."

The three of them went to work. Feed... crank... shake out... pin on the clothesline... feed... crank... shake out—

"What's this?" cried Lilly suddenly, shaking out a crisp, white pillowcase. Two holes gaped in the material. "Buddy! Did you tear this pillowcase with that stick?" she wailed, alarmed. "This is a brand new customer! City councilman's wife, too! If she find out we ruined her pillowcase, why, she probably pass word round town, and I'll lose all my customers!"

"Mama, let me see that," said Celeste, snatching the wet pillowcase out of her mother's hands. Celeste looked closely at the holes. They weren't torn... cut, more likely. The holes were even, side by side. If a man put that pillowcase over his head, the holes would just about line up with—

"Eyeholes!" gasped Celeste, starting to tremble. In her mind, she saw white-robed figures on horseback in the woods, without faces, only... eyeholes. "Who sent you this laundry, Mama?" she demanded.

"Why, lady by the name of Rogers—city councilman's wife, I think she said." Lilly's eyes searched Celeste's face anxiously. "What you mean, 'eyeholes,' girl?"

Celeste sank down onto the ground and hugged her knees. She remembered the rude city councilman who wouldn't tip his hat to Mrs. Bethune. "Oh, Mama, they're here... the Ku Klux Klan. Here in Daytona, too."

Chapter 9

The Turpentine Mission

MARY BETHUNE PURSED HER LIPS thoughtfully as Celeste poured out the story of the pillowcase with eyeholes—and an eyebrow went up when Celeste mentioned the name of the laundry's owner.

"Rogers, hmmm... I think we've met the man," she said with a wry smile. "Celeste, the Bible tells us to be wise as serpents and harmless as doves. There's nothing we can do right now about what you've discovered, except to be alert and to pray. Remember our motto, child: Victory through prayer! This hate group is probably very small—too few and too cowardly to do anything but make themselves feel big and

important by sneaking around at night and scaring people."

Celeste cried, "But in Statesboro the Klan—!"

"This isn't Georgia," Mary Bethune said firmly. "This is Daytona, Florida, and we have many friends here. Now come on, child. We still have a lot of work to do clearing the dump and raising money before the carpenters can start building Faith Hall."

✧ ✧ ✧ ✧

Faith Hall was dedicated the following year. People all over Daytona were amazed at the large four-story, white-frame building. Over the entryway a wooden plaque declared, "Enter to Learn." On the other side of the doorway a similar plaque declared, "Depart to Serve."

"How did you do it?" Mrs. Bethune was asked over and over. And her answer was always the same: "The Lord just helped us pray up, sing up, and talk up this building!"

Many people, both black and white, filled the auditorium, and the choir sang—almost two hundred voices strong. In the haunting spirituals and uplifting gospel music, Celeste was able to drown out the voices of fear and replace them—if only briefly—with voices of faith.

But fear still dogged her, raising its head the day the Ku Klux Klan marched down Main Street in Daytona with signs that said "Niggers Go Home" and "Daytona Is for Whites." There were only a handful of men dressed in their white robes and makeshift hoods, but the crowd along the sidewalk was silent. No sweet potato pies were delivered that day.

And the fear was there when signs began appearing in downtown Daytona. Certain taxis were posted "Whites Only." "Colored—Carryout Only," said a sign in a restaurant window. Soon the signs were everywhere: a "White" water fountain and a "Colored" water spigot nearby; "White" benches and "Colored" benches; "White" windows at the post office and "Black" windows.

"Why are they doing this?" the girls demanded of Mrs. Bethune as they gathered in Faith Hall for a school assembly. "It wasn't like this before!"

"They're called Jim Crow laws," Mrs. Bethune explained sadly, her face troubled. "Jim Crow was a character from old minstrel shows where a white actor dressed up like an old slave and made fun of black people. Jim Crow laws are designed to keep blacks and whites separate from each other, to make sure the black man remains a second-class citizen. Jim Crow laws have been creeping through all the southern states... and now they're the law here in Florida, too."

Celeste covered her ears. *Why? Why? Why?*

"But not at this school," Mrs. Bethune continued. "Here every person is a first-class citizen. If you are a student or teacher of this school, you will continue to treat every person—black or white, rich or poor—as a first-class citizen. We mustn't allow misguided white folks to rob us of our dignity, our freedom, or our citizenship."

Celeste uncovered her ears. Mrs. Bethune's voice was no longer sad but strong. Her chin was up; her eyes were flashing. "Our choir is very popular with blacks and whites alike. I think it's time we invite people to hear us sing in our own auditorium. Sunday afternoons we will give community concerts. No segregation allowed. If people want to come, it will be black and white together. That is the vision on which this school was founded, and that is the vision—"

The rest of her sentence was drowned out in the thunderous applause and cheers of over two hundred girls and teachers.

✧ ✧ ✧ ✧

"Do I look all right?" Celeste asked Lena nervously. They were sitting in the front of the auditorium, waiting anxiously to be called to the front to receive their certificate of graduation from eighth grade.

"You look any more all right, you gonna knock 'em dead," said Lena jealously. Celeste at thirteen was already blossoming into young womanhood, while Lena still had the gawky look of a twelve-year-old.

Daytona Educational and Industrial Institute was honoring its first eighth-grade graduating class. Several more buildings had been built on the property, and an abundant garden across the street produced not only food for the school, but a popular vegetable stand selling "the freshest vegetables in Daytona" to the local population.

Celeste glanced back at the rows of parents and onlookers and saw her parents. They were proud of her, she knew, but even though the school had been growing and thriving, things hadn't been going well for the Key family and other blacks in Shanty Town. The railroad jobs had finally ended. Samuel and Tom found work at a nearby rock quarry, but the work was hard and dangerous.

Other families weren't even that fortunate. The only other work available was deep in the pine forests where pine pitch was distilled into turpentine. Make-shift camps had grown up around these turpentine distilleries, but Celeste had heard her mama say, "I pray to God ever' day that you don't lose that quarry job, Samuel. This shanty town be poor enough, but I hear folks be livin' like animals out there in those turpentine camps!"

Celeste shivered. She didn't know what her mama meant, and she didn't want to know, either. Living under Mrs. Bethune's oversight, she had grown to appreciate the school's standards for cleanliness and good manners, as well as the exposure to books, music, and art. In fact, she'd been working so hard to keep her grades up and stay in school so she could sing in the choir, that she hadn't given one minute's thought to what was going to happen after graduation.

But now here it was. And suddenly Celeste's excitement gave way to a horrible thought. Was this her last day at Daytona Educational? Whatever was she going to do now if she couldn't go to school? Endless days of helping Mama do the washing for white folks or taking care of five-year-old Button suddenly loomed before her.

Lena poked her in the ribs. "Listen!" she hissed.

"...so I am pleased to announce that we will be adding the first year of high school to our next school term," Mrs. Bethune was saying. "And a generous benefactor—who wishes to remain anonymous—has set aside tuition money for any of our graduates today who wish to continue their education at Daytona Educational and Industrial School."

The announcement was met with "Hallelujahs!" and a standing ovation, but no one leaped to her feet faster or clapped louder than Celeste Key. *Saved*, she thought with relief, *from endless days of drudgery*!

✧ ✧ ✧ ✧

With her upper arm, Celeste tried to wipe away the sweat dripping from her forehead down her nose while her hands were plunged into soapy dishwater in the school kitchen. She stared resentfully at a neatly lettered sign over the kitchen sink: "Cease to be a drudge; seek to be an artist."

Celeste rolled her eyes. Sometimes Mrs. Bethune's persistent cheerfulness about work was just too much.

"Hey, aren't you done yet?" Lena poked her head into the kitchen. "Come on! I just volunteered us to go with Mrs. Bethune on a ride to inspect the turpentine camps. But we have to go right now!"

"The turpentine camps!" snorted Celeste. "I don't want to—" She stopped herself. A ride in Mrs. Bethune's buggy into the shady forest on a hot summer Saturday would be fun. And if they were only going to *look*, and not *stay* there...

Even the cook was surprised at how quickly slowpoke Celeste Key finished up the last of the breakfast dishes and was out the door.

Mrs. Bethune's bicycle for getting around town had been replaced by a sturdy two-seater buggy and a gentle brown mare. Ten-year-old Albert was on the driver's seat with his mother, and Celeste climbed into the second seat with Lena and two other girls, Eugenia and Shadie.

They drove out of town, passing buckboards and mules, as well as several of those new Model-T Ford motorcars that were so popular with the white tourists. The drivers thought it great sport to blow their horns and spook the horses, but Albert's firm hand on the reins kept the brown mare on the road.

The road into the pine forest was rutted and narrow. The girls squealed as the buggy bumped over tree roots and down into potholes. On and on they went, deeper into the cool shade and pungent smell of the longleaf pines. Suddenly Mrs. Bethune said, "Stop here."

Celeste looked around, bewildered. A camp of

ramshackle lean-tos and huts seemed to appear out of nowhere. Rotting garbage and pigs made the air smell foul. A couple of men lounged on the ground, passing a dark brown bottle among them. Children appeared and gaped at the visitors, most of them dirty from head to toe, many of them with runny noses and matted hair.

"You girls make friends with the children," Mrs. Bethune ordered. "I'm going to find their parents."

Make friends—! Celeste didn't even want to get down from the buggy, much less talk to the little urchins. But Lena gave her a look, so she climbed down and followed Albert and the other girls. The camp children grabbed their hands and seemed eager for attention, but Celeste pulled her hands away.

No telling what disease a person could get touching these children.

She could see Mrs. Bethune going from hut to hut, disappearing inside or talking in the doorway to a woman who usually had a baby on her hip. The teacher paused and talked a long time to the idle men. There was a lot of gesturing, and Celeste wondered impatiently how long this was going to take.

Finally Mrs. Bethune came striding back to the buggy, her mouth set firmly. As Albert turned the buggy around and they bounced back along the forest road the way they had come, Mrs. Bethune blurted out angrily, "These turpentine camps! Why, conditions here are worse than slavery fifty years ago. Lord have mercy! At least slave owners made an effort to keep their slaves healthy because they had paid out good money for them. But here!" She threw up her hands. "Workers are a dime a dozen. If one man gets hurt or sick, there are three more waiting to take his place. Why, those huts wouldn't even keep the pigs dry, much less a family with babies."

Celeste couldn't remember seeing Mrs. Bethune so upset—not even when that ignorant old woman said Negro people couldn't learn past third grade.

"One mother said they'd buried three children just in the last two months," Mrs. Bethune went on. "There are no stores, no churches, no doctors, no schools . . . no wonder the men lay around half drunk, and the children are sick."

Celeste silently agreed. It was an awful place, and personally she never wanted to see it again.

But the very next Saturday, a reluctant Celeste found herself in the back of a wagon, filled with girls and teachers from the school, plus buckets, soap, scrub brushes, medicines, fresh vegetables from the school garden, hand-me-down clothes collected from neighbors, and storybooks. Mrs. Bethune and the teachers went from hut to hut, sending any available man to the creek for water and helping the women scrub down furniture and floors. Meanwhile, the schoolgirls bathed children, dressed them in clean clothes, then read stories to them while the house-cleaning went on.

The very next day, Sunday, Mrs. Bethune was back with her Bible. The girls came, too, and sang the beautiful spirituals, then Mrs. Bethune preached from John 3:16. "'Whosoever' means you!" she pleaded. "God sent His Son to show you how much you are worth to Him!"

The next week they came again. Fires were built; tubs were filled with water; bedding was washed, rinsed, and hung on bushes to dry. Small noses were wiped, ears were scrubbed, hair was washed and braided, followed by preaching and singing on Sunday.

And then it was on to the next camp. "Our 'Turpentine Mission,'" Mrs. Bethune called her new summer project.

Why does Mrs. Bethune think she has to save the world? Celeste thought grumpily as another Saturday dawned and the long trip to the turpentine camps loomed before her. Maybe it would be all right if they just stayed at one camp and had gotten to enjoy the improvements—but it was always on to another camp, usually smellier and dirtier and more disgusting than the last one.

"I'm not feeling so good," she complained to one of the teachers. The teacher was distracted and simply said she must then stay in bed and rest. Hardly daring to believe her good fortune, Celeste curled up in the quiet dormitory room with a book and was just congratulating herself on what she considered a well-deserved day of rest, when Mrs. Bethune marched into the room, took her by the hand, and marched her out to the waiting wagons.

"Don't pull that one again, young lady," she said sternly. "What you have been given you have to give back. Are you forgetting what it says over the doorway of Faith Hall? 'Enter to learn . . . depart to serve.' We're not free until all are free."

Celeste's face burned. Instead of feeling repentant, the task ahead just seemed all the more distasteful. *I thought getting an education meant a person could better herself and walk among the best of society—not get stuck in these trash-hole turpentine camps! she seethed to herself.*

Her job that morning was hauling water and scrubbing out yet another filthy shack. As she struggled back to the camp with the heavy, sloshing bucket, she saw a bush dripping with huckleberries, small and dusty blue. Now that was a treat! She plucked a handful and popped them in her mouth, relishing the tangy juice. Another mouthful, and another . . . until finally she picked up the bucket and reluctantly headed back to the camp.

On the way home that afternoon, Celeste began to feel strange. She had a sharp pain in her belly, but she didn't dare say anything to anyone, or Mrs. Bethune would think she was just trying to get out of coming back the next day. The pain sharpened during the night, and Celeste threw up into an old basin. *There*, she thought with relief, *that ought to take care of those old huckleberries.*

But the pain was still there in the morning. Gritting her teeth, she held on to the jolting wagon as they went back to yesterday's camp to "have church," as Mrs. Bethune called it.

"Are you all right, girl?" Lena asked, looking at Celeste suspiciously as they climbed back into the wagons to go home. Celeste licked her lips and nodded.

But that night in bed, the pain was so intense that Celeste moaned into her pillow and tossed and turned. Alarmed, Lena hunted up a teacher, who felt Celeste's damp, feverish face and went running to awaken Mrs. Bethune.

Taking one look at Celeste, Mrs. Bethune pulled up the girl's nightshirt and felt her belly. "Aaaahhh!" Celeste cried out, as fingers touched her swollen right side.

"She said it was huckleberries," said the teacher. "She was afraid to tell us, afraid we'd think—"

"This isn't huckleberries," said Mrs. Bethune grimly. "I might be wrong, but if I were a betting woman, I'd put my money on appendicitis. We've got to get this girl to a doctor—right now!"

Chapter 10

Pallet in the Pantry

THE BROWN MARE WAS HITCHED UP to Mary Bethune's buggy, and Mrs. Bethune herself drove quickly through the warm summer night while Frances Keyser cradled a moaning Celeste in the backseat.

"Where are we going to find a doctor at this time of night?" Mrs. Keyser worried as the buggy turned at first one street and then another. "This child is starting to run a fever... what?" The teacher recognized where they were going. "Mary McLeod Bethune, what are you doing? The hospital won't take this girl! Don't you remember what happened when you broke your arm?"

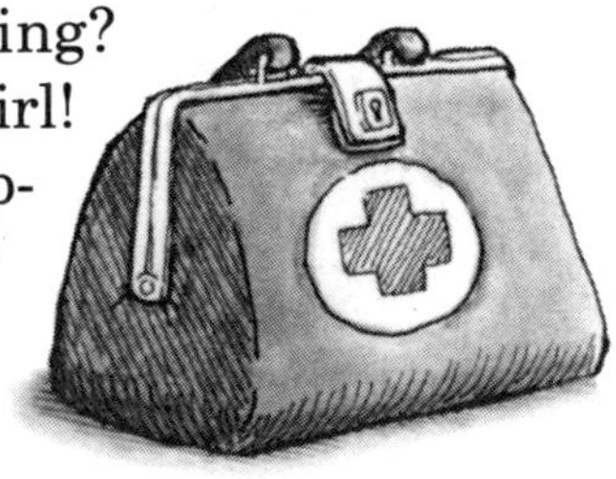

Mrs. Bethune just slapped

the reins on the mare's back to keep the horse at a fast trot. "We have no choice," she said grimly. "She's going to need an operation—fast."

Celeste's fever was beginning to rise, and she had to grit her teeth against the pain caused by the jostling buggy. Finally the horse and buggy stopped in front of a square, white building, but she was only slightly aware of a pounding on a door and then voices arguing in the night.

"What's the meaning of all this racket? Our patients are asleep!" said a stern, woman's voice.

"We need a doctor—quickly! This young girl—"

"Sorry. This hospital doesn't take Negro patients."

"It does now," said Mrs. Bethune's voice firmly. "This girl will die if her appendix bursts!"

"It's hospital policy," said the voice. "Whites only."

"Get a doctor—*now*!" said Mrs. Bethune, her voice rising in anger. "I will not leave until I see a doctor!"

Celeste moaned on the buggy seat. The front door slammed in the quiet night, and footsteps faded inside. Mary Bethune and Frances Keyser whispered together.

"They won't come back!" the younger teacher said. "We're wasting time—we have to find a black doctor. I heard there was one up in—"

"There isn't time," retorted Mrs. Bethune. "That's forty—maybe fifty miles away. Celeste needs a doctor now!"

The whispered arguing continued, then the door opened again. "What do you want?" asked a young male voice.

"Are you a doctor? This girl has appendicitis. She needs help right away!"

"I'm sorry." The voice sounded tired, irritated. "Our head nurse has already explained to you—"

"Sir! I am Mrs. Mary McLeod Bethune, principal of the Daytona Educational and Industrial Institute. We have many prominent white businessmen on our Board of Trustees. If you refuse to help this girl... if she dies because of your neglect... I will publicize this incident to the full extent of my—"

"All right, all right," said the voice. "Drive the buggy around to the back of the hospital. I'll meet you at the door."

Celeste, lying on the buggy seat with her eyes squeezed shut, felt the buggy jostle again. She was scared. The pain was almost unbearable... but she didn't want to be left at a white hospital that didn't want her.

Frances Keyser and Mary Bethune helped her out of the buggy and into a small, dark hallway at the back of the hospital. The young doctor, his white coat rumpled as if he'd been sleeping in it, met them with a wooden chair on wheels. "I'll take her from here," he said sharply, helping them seat Celeste in the chair.

"Don't leave me!" Celeste cried out, feeling panic rising in her throat. She reached out a hand to the familiar, comforting figures at her side.

"She wants us to stay—" started Mrs. Bethune.

"Leave her!" the doctor snapped. "I'm going

against policy as it is. I can't have you colored women sitting around the halls calling attention to her presence. Now go—you can return tomorrow night. Come to the back door."

Celeste felt the chair start to move down the dark hall. Hot tears of pain and fear slid down her cheeks as she gripped the arms of the wheeled chair. A familiar voice floated after her.

"Be brave, Celeste! You are in God's hands. Remember, victory through prayer!"

✧ ✧ ✧ ✧

Celeste awoke in a strange, tiny room. She was lying on the floor on a thin pallet. Where was she? What was she doing here? Frightened, she tried to get up, but immediately she felt faint, and a sharp pain stabbed her side. Now she remembered... the ride in the wheeled chair down the dark hallway... being lifted onto a tall, narrow bed... strange white faces staring at her... whispered comments she couldn't hear... then the funny mask they put over her nose and that awful, sharp smell....

She fell back onto the pallet and looked around anxiously. She was in some sort of kitchen pantry with a door at one end and a narrow window at the other. Tall shelves went from floor to ceiling on either side, and large cans, jars, and sacks of food crowded every inch of shelf space.

Twisting her head, she could see out the open door of the pantry. She heard the sound of voices

and pots and pans banging. The smell of food cooking made her stomach feel queasy.

Someone came into the pantry—a white girl with a sharp nose and pale eyes. She made a big show of having to step around Celeste's pallet to get a large jar of canned tomatoes. "As if my job ain't hard enough," she muttered sourly, "without them sticking patients in the pantry—and a colored one at that." She glared at Celeste. "You ain't 'sposed to be here, ya know."

Celeste's eyes filled with tears as the cook's assistant left. She wanted to go home. She wanted her mama... or Mrs. Bethune... or even her sister, Lucy.

The hours dragged on. Once, the young doctor stopped by, checked the dressing covering the surgical wound on her belly, and left without speaking. Then the little room began to get dark. The noises in the kitchen finally died down. Celeste was scared. She didn't want to stay in this tiny room all night in the dark! Her mouth felt dry, and suddenly all she could think about was a drink of water.

After a while she heard hushed voices. "She's in here" came the young doctor's voice. And suddenly Mrs. Bethune was kneeling down at her side.

"Oh, you've come! You've come!" cried Celeste, and she burst into grateful sobs.

"Hush, now, hush," soothed Mrs. Bethune. Then she stood up. "What is the meaning of this?" she said angrily. "A pallet in the pantry? Surely this hospital isn't that crowded."

"Look, auntie, I've gone against policy as it is. You can't expect—"

"Auntie?" said Mrs. Bethune. A note of amused annoyance crept into her voice. "Which one my brother's children are you?"

Celeste looked up at the young doctor. His mouth dropped open, and for a moment he seemed at a loss for words. "Just-just get her out of here," he finally sputtered. "I'll send the bill to the school."

A short while later, Celeste gratefully lay against Frances Keyser on the buggy seat. Mrs. Bethune, still angry, sent the horse and buggy flying through the dark streets, until Mrs. Keyser protested. "Easy! We don't want the stitches to tear open."

The horse settled down to an even trot, but Mrs. Bethune's thoughts were still racing. "We need our own hospital," she said abruptly. "We need our own doctor, we need to be training nurses in our school... now!"

✧ ✧ ✧ ✧

"You mean she actually said, 'Which one of my brother's children are you?'—*to his face*?" Lena said incredulously.

Celeste was enjoying the luxury of a day of complete rest, and Lena had dropped in to keep her company and hear all the details of her adventure from start to finish.

Celeste nodded, and the two girls dissolved into helpless laughter. "Oh! Oh, don't," gasped Celeste, holding her side. "It hurts to laugh."

"Glad to hear you're feeling better," said a familiar voice. Mrs. Bethune came into the dormitory room and sat down on the bed. Still giggling, Lena excused herself and went back to her afternoon chores.

Mrs. Bethune got right to the point. "Celeste, I have decided to add practical nursing to our high school curriculum. I would like you to consider taking the course. We will need nurses for our new hospital."

"Me! A nurse!" Celeste had never really thought seriously about what she wanted to do with her education. But nursing—surely that would be a lot of hard work. She tried to think of an excuse. "But... but I've been thinking about being a teacher, like you."

Mrs. Bethune smiled at Celeste's sudden desire to follow in her footsteps, but said, "You will have to love learning more than you show right now to be a teacher," she said. "There is time to make a final decision, but I would like you to give the nursing program a try. You are brighter than you give yourself credit for. But you need to work. *Use* the talents God has given you, Celeste—use them to help your people."

Alone once more, Celeste lay back and looked out the open window at the large oak trees shading the school. She was surprised that Mrs. Bethune would ask her to try the new nursing program, given all the struggles she'd had sticking to her studies. But she felt pleased, too. If Mrs. Bethune believed in her, maybe... well, she could at least try.

✧ ✧ ✧ ✧

With the help of Mr. Gamble, Mr. White, and others on the Board of Trustees, Mary McLeod Bethune lost no time searching for a young, promising Negro doctor who would be willing to come to Daytona. "Hallelujah!" she cried when a letter finally arrived from a recent medical school graduate, saying he would very much like to come and agreed to the terms offered. It was signed, "Dr. Henry Jackson."

Hundreds of letters were sent out to raise money to purchase a cottage near the school, which was then set up as a two-bed hospital. And when the new high school curriculum was established, it included a full range of academics, household economy, dressmaking, dairy and poultry farming, gardening, rug weaving . . . and practical nursing.

Albertus Bethune arrived on one of his visits for the dedication of the little hospital. So did Mary Bethune's mother, Patsy McLeod: great-granddaughter of an African prince, former slave, and mother of seventeen children. It was the first time the work-worn, seventy-year-old woman had ever ridden on a train or seen her eleven-year-old grandson. Tears of pride and joy glistened on Mrs. Bethune's face as she told her mother's story and then announced the name of the new building: McLeod Hospital.

Albertus and Mary Bethune decided to send young Albert to Haines Institute, which was coeducational, in Augusta, Georgia, and the visitors went back to Georgia with him. Then it was back to another busy year at Daytona Educational.

Two hospital beds weren't very many, but it was two more than Daytona's black community had had before. As the money was raised, more beds and medical equipment were added, and young Dr. Jackson was kept busy treating everything from fevers and broken legs to pneumonia and stomach tumors. And the girls who had signed up for the course in practical nursing were getting a close-up idea of what "practical" meant.

"Huh!" muttered Celeste to herself as she carried a bedpan out of the hospital cottage and dumped its contents down the hole of the outhouse in back. It was May, and the subtropical "winter" was heating up toward summer. She was almost finished with her first year of high school, and she had been trying, she really had, she told herself. But sometimes the complaints just came spilling out. "Wash the bedding, make the beds, give bed baths, hold screaming kids while they get shots, empty bedpans, scrub the floors," she grumbled. "Might as well be raising a bunch of kids."

Helping Dr. Jackson with "medical stuff" was a little more interesting. She learned how to change dressings, sterilize surgical instruments, and check a patient's vital signs. But even that lost its glamor. Many of the people who needed medical attention had disgusting problems like neglected, runny sores and "the runs." Dr. Jackson often shook his head over diseases or injuries that had been neglected too long.

Back in the hospital cottage, Celeste rinsed out

the bedpan, washed her hands, and put her apron in the dirty clothes. Good, her afternoon shift was over. As she walked back toward the school campus—the old town dump that was sprouting new buildings slowly but surely—she mentally rehearsed her speech for Mrs. Bethune. "Mrs. Bethune, I appreciate your giving me the opportunity to study nursing, but I'd like to switch to dressmaking. I really think I'd be good at designing women's hats—"

Celeste stopped short. Two wagons and teams of horses were coming wildly down the road. A black man was driving the first team, with a white man sitting grimly beside him, hanging on to his hat. The wagons thundered past her, and the white man yelled at her, "Get help! Explosion at—" But the rest of his words were drowned out by the thundering hooves and rattling wagons.

Celeste ran into Faith Hall. "Emergency!" she cried. "Emergency! They need help at the hospital!" Teachers and staff people came running. Soon volunteers were surrounding the wagons, carrying badly injured men into the little hospital.

With a sense of dread, Celeste made her way into the waiting room of the cottage. Men, covered with blood and dirt, with hideous wounds on faces, chests, and legs, were propped against the walls or laid out, unconscious, on the floor. There were too many! This little hospital couldn't take care of them all! Celeste felt like running away, shutting out the groans of pain, but she knew all nursing students would be needed to help.

"Explosion at the rock quarry," the white man was saying to Dr. Jackson. His clothes were spattered with blood—the blood of other men. "I'm sure glad you people built this hospital. I didn't know where else to get help for my colored boys. I can't afford to lose too many of 'em."

Rock quarry? Celeste froze.

Dr. Jackson and the white quarry boss picked up one of the unconscious men and carried him into the surgery room. "Celeste!" barked the Negro doctor. "I need you to clean off the blood and dirt from this man so I can attend to his wounds—quickly!"

The left side of the big man's face and muscular body was mangled almost beyond recognition. Trembling, Celeste quickly got a basin of clean water. As she turned toward the man on the operating table, his eyes fluttered open and he looked right at her.

"Celeste... help me," the man whispered hoarsely.

Celeste felt the blood drain from her face.

It was her father.

Chapter 11

Student Nurse

AT FIRST GLANCE, the Negro man entering the crowded waiting room of McLeod Hospital seemed old and frail. He used a cane to steady the limp on his left side. His clothes hung on his thin body, and his nappy hair was "salt-and-pepper." Scars laced the left side of his face and neck and disappeared into the collar of his shirt.

As the man sat down in a wooden chair and picked up a newspaper, a young woman of nineteen in a long, light blue dress with white apron and white cap came into the room and stopped in surprise.

"Papa!" she said, breaking

into a smile. "I didn't know you were coming in today."

The man was frowning over the newspaper and didn't seem to hear. Quickly, the young woman crossed the room and spoke into his good ear. "Hey, Papa, how're you doing?"

Samuel Key looked up, and his troubled face lit up in a smile. "Hey, baby," he said. "I'm doin' pretty good. Just coming in for my April checkup with Dr. Jackson. That left hip of mine been bothering me again. Still, can't complain."

It had been five years since the explosion in the rock quarry. Samuel Key was only fifty-three, but he looked ten years older. The explosion had left him blind in his left eye, deaf in his left ear, and he walked with a limp. But it was true: He wasn't complaining. Without McLeod Hospital, he and many others would have died.

All over the world things were happening. Woodrow Wilson was elected President of the United States in 1912, and again in 1916.... The wars raging in Europe threatened to explode into a world-wide war, but so far the United States had stayed neutral.... Booker T. Washington, founder of Tuskegee Institute, died in 1915—the same year the state of Georgia gave a legal charter to the "new" Ku Klux Klan.

Things were happening on Second Avenue in Daytona, Florida, too. McLeod Hospital had grown to twenty beds and had added more doctors. Each fall another year was added to the high school program at

Daytona Educational and Industrial Institute, and then two years of junior college. The "Turpentine Missions," begun the summer of 1911, had become a regular part of Mrs. Bethune's community outreach; many of her students got "teacher training" by teaching school for the children in the turpentine camps for three months each summer. Mrs. Bethune had gotten word by letter that her husband, Albertus, had become ill and died. But, in spite of Jim Crow laws and occasional bullying from the local Ku Klux Klan, the school was growing and generally respected.

Samuel Key looked his daughter up and down. "Look at you," he beamed again. "Can't for the life of me figure out what made you decide to become a nurse, but here you are, all growed up and a nurse, too."

Celeste pushed her father playfully. "You know good and well what made me decide to be a nurse! How else was I going to take care of you and nurse you back to health after that awful explosion at the quarry? But I'm not a nurse yet—still got a couple more years of college."

"You coming by the house tonight for supper?" asked Celeste's father hopefully. "Seems like it gets harder an' harder to get the family all together, now that Lucy's got herself a husband and a young'un of her own, and Tom working himself to death at the quarry—thinks he has to make up for what I can't do."

"Sorry, Papa. I have choir practice tonight. Maybe

tomorrow, all right?" She hesitated. "Is Tom… I mean—"

"Mr. Key?" interrupted a voice. It was one of the staff nurses looking at the next appointment in the book.

Samuel Key put down the newspaper and got stiffly to his feet. Celeste watched him limp into the

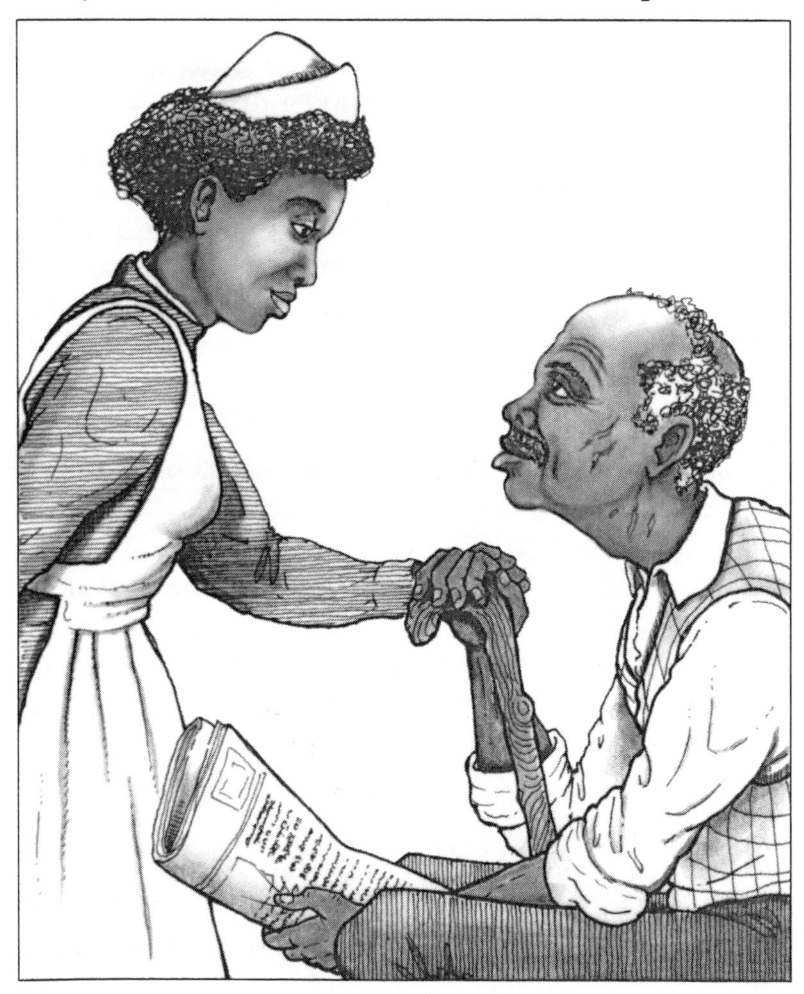

examining room, his once tall, muscular body now slightly bent and much thinner. Seeing her own father, all mangled and bloody, on the operating table that day had been a turning point for Celeste. The white hospital wouldn't have taken all those wounded colored men. What if there hadn't been a McLeod Hospital? Her father would have died.

Suddenly, dirty bedpans and washing hospital bed sheets had seemed like nothing compared to staying by his side, changing the dressings on his wounds twice a day, spooning water through his dry lips. Celeste was glad she had something to do, something that could help.

There were many other wounded and dying men that day. Days blurred into nights; all the young student nurses were called on to work double shifts. But Mrs. Bethune was right there to encourage them. "Pray!" she said. "Work! Your help comes from the Lord. Do what you can and leave the rest in God's hands."

For the first time, Celeste discovered what it meant to "lean on the Lord." She prayed and worked and prayed some more. And then there was that glad day when her father walked out of the hospital and back to his family—a little blind, a little deaf, a little crippled . . . but *alive* and well again. She could almost hear Mrs. Bethune's booming voice in her head: *"Victory through prayer!"*

Even her teachers noticed the difference in Celeste's attitude. The girl who was always looking for an excuse to get out of work settled down and tackled her books with a new seriousness. Celeste couldn't really explain it. But things Mrs. Bethune had been trying to teach her from the first day of school suddenly seemed to make sense. If that "whosoever" in John 3:16 really meant her, Celeste thought to herself, and if God loved her enough to give His own Son *for her*, then maybe it was time she gave something back to God and to her own people.

As the examining room door shut behind her father, Celeste shook off her thoughts and got up. Right now she had hospital rounds to make, checking on patients. She was looking forward to choir practice tonight. The rich spirituals and gospel music had become the best way she knew to express the hope that grows out of despair.

But as she got up, her eyes fell on the newspaper her father had been reading. The headline was bold and black across the top of the paper:

**UNITED STATES DECLARES
WAR ON GERMANY!**

✧ ✧ ✧ ✧

The news about the United States entering the war in Europe traveled like wildfire through Daytona. People were mad that unarmed U.S. cargo and passenger ships had been torpedoed by German submarines. Men and boys were leaving their jobs and eagerly lining up to volunteer for the army.

As Celeste walked home the next evening to have

supper with her family, she wondered anxiously what it all meant. Daytona, Florida, was right on the coast . . . would the war come to this side of the ocean? to their very own town?

She walked up the path to the house. The Key shanty had gradually grown into a sturdy, if somewhat jumbled, house with wooden floors, additional rooms, and a front porch. But heat and cooking were still done by woodburning stoves, lights were oil lamps, plumbing was an outhouse, and they carried their own trash to the dump because Daytona's electric company and other city services didn't include Shanty Town.

Samuel Key, Tom, and seventeen-year-old Buddy were arguing on the front porch as Celeste drew near. "Volunteer? You gotta be out of your mind, Papa," Tom was saying bitterly. "This ain't my war. I ain't got no beef with no Germans—'cept they be white men. Far as I can see, ain't no difference between white folks over there and white folks over here. Let 'em fight it out with each other."

"I'll go, Papa," Buddy piped up eagerly. "Man, get to ride on one of them big ships, see the world, get my own gun—" Buddy peered down the sights on an imaginary rifle and made shooting noises.

"You ain't old enough yet," said Samuel Key, dismissing Buddy's annoying noises with a wave of his hand. "Gotta be eighteen. And this family ain't sending no boy when we got a full-grown man to do a man's job." He jabbed a finger at Tom's chest. "The United States is your country, Tom Key, whether you like it or not. This is where you was born, this is where you gonna live—God willin'—another fifty, sixty years, this is where you gonna be buried. It's your duty to defend it."

Startled, Celeste stopped at the corner of the porch. Tom go to war? It had never occurred to her that black boys would sign up for the army. Policemen and soldiers in the South had always been white—and black folks had better say, "Yes, sir," and look at the ground humble-like to someone in a uniform.

"*Defend* it?" Tom laughed bitterly. "What did this country ever do for me? My grandpappy was a *slave*—or is you forgettin' that already, Papa? The good citizens of Statesboro burned your blacksmith shop down, Papa—or is you forgettin' that, too? Only jobs we can get round here be breakin' our backs, doing what nobody else wants to do. Even our mama breakin' *her* back 'cause white folks don't wanna wash they own dirty clothes."

Celeste held her breath. She had never heard Tom talk to their father like this. Even Buddy was staring at his older brother in shock.

"And look at you!" Tom continued. "Big, strappin' man like you, old before your time because them quarry bosses be takin' shortcuts all the time, not thinkin' 'bout the safety of their workers."

Celeste saw her father wince as Tom scratched open the wounds of painful memories. But when Samuel Key spoke, his voice was steady.

"I ain't forgettin', son. No way I can forget. But that ain't the point. The laws of this country say we's citizens with rights and responsibilities—"

"Huh!" snorted Tom, shaking his head angrily. "Bunch of lies."

"Now you listen!" snapped Samuel. "I hear what you saying. This country don't always live up to its own laws; that true. But it's time we Negroes lived up to our rights and responsibilities instead of waiting for whites to allow it."

Celeste was tempted to laugh. She could almost hear Mrs. Bethune's voice teaching the regular evening civics classes.

Tom recognized it, too. "Now you're sounding like that schoolteacher woman."

"So what if I do?" said Samuel. "It's true. This country will become what we make it become. It's come a long way, and it's got a long way to go. But we can't give up now. We gotta vote; we gotta fight; we gotta stand up for what's right." The former blacksmith pounded the porch railing with each point. "And I don't want no white bigot or Ku Kluxer saying a few years down the line that we don't have no right to vote 'cause we didn't fight when our country went to war."

Tom just shook his head, but Celeste could tell their father's words had made a point.

Just then Lilly Key came to the open front door, wiping her hands on her apron. "Well, if you menfolk are gonna vote or fight, you better off doin' it on a full stomach—why, if it ain't Celeste! Why didn't anybody tell me Celeste had come already? Come on, now, everybody. . . ."

✧ ✧ ✧ ✧

The Key family stood on the train platform in Daytona as the giant oil-burning steam locomotive puffed into view. Scores of young army recruits—mostly white—were standing with their families, ready to board the train for Fort Benning, Georgia.

Tom stood slightly apart, and Celeste wondered what was going through his mind. Everything had happened so fast, and now Tom was leaving. Leaving... to what?

Ever since she could remember, her older brother had been doing a man's job. It was he who had gone with his mother that fateful day back in Statesboro—gone into danger and almost didn't make it back home alive. He had worked alongside his father on the railroad, then the rock quarry.

Now he was going off to war. Celeste couldn't imagine war. But she knew many men would be wounded, many would die, and many would never come home.

She was frightened for Tom but tried not to show it for her mother's sake.

"All aboard!" yelled the conductor.

There were hugs and tears. Celeste dared a quick hug, and to her surprise, Tom hugged her back. "Go with God," she whispered in his ear. A lump swelled in her throat.

The young men began to shuffle onto the train, Tom with them. Suddenly there was a loud, harsh voice just behind them.

“What do you think you’re doing, boy?” yelled a voice. Celeste whirled and saw a familiar figure—Mr. Rogers, the city councilman. “You can’t get on that car,” the man said, glaring at Tom. “The colored car is at the end of the train. Can’t you read?”

Celeste’s head jerked toward the train car in front of them. Sure enough, a small sign was posted in the window: “Whites Only.”

“Don’t know why the gov’ment allows colored soldiers, anyway,” the man muttered.

Tom didn’t look at Mr. Rogers. But Celeste saw the seething bitterness in his eyes just before his face went blank, like a closed book—a look that made her want to cry out in pain. Without a word Tom swung his pack onto his shoulder and headed for the end of the train.

Celeste turned away, hot tears blinding her eyes. Racism was already killing her brother. Racism, and now war. Would they ever see Tom alive again?

Chapter 12

Turn on the Lights!

CELESTE PEDDLED THE BICYCLE down the dirt road of Shanty Town and braked to an awkward stop at the path leading up to her family's house. "Mama!" she called, running up the steps to the front porch. "Mama! I've got good news!"

Lilly Key met her at the front door, eyes wide. "Tom?" she asked eagerly.

Celeste shook her head. "No, I'm sorry, Mama. I didn't mean to get your hopes up—" She stopped as her mother's face fell.

"That's all right, honey," Lilly sighed. "But it's been months since the war ended. I thought he'd be home by now, or we'd hear *somethin'*."

"I know, Mama." It was hard

waiting and wondering. But the excitement over her own news still bubbled inside. She glanced around. "Is Papa home? I want to tell you both my good news."

"No, he off with Button, trying to get the boy 'prenticed to Jake Williams, the blacksmith where your papa been working part time. My, my," Lilly wagged her head. "My baby off gettin' a job."

"Mama! Your 'baby' is fourteen years old," teased Celeste. "Wish he could keep goin' to school, but... I understand. Times are hard. We've all got to help make ends meet. And that"—her eyes danced mischievously—"is part of my good news! Oh, Mama... they're going to hire me full time at McLeod Hospital now that I'm graduating! I'll be making a real salary!"

"Why, girl, that's wonderful—"

"And that's not all, Mama!" Celeste rushed on. "Mrs. Bethune asked if I would take over the choir—lead it, Mama! I'm so excited, I can hardly breathe! Why, all along I've been thinking that I'd have to leave the choir now that I'm graduating. But, as choir director—"

A shout from outside the house interrupted Celeste's news. "Lilly! Come quick! We need help here!" It was her father's voice.

With a startled glance at each other, mother and daughter both rushed for the door. Celeste stared in astonishment. Her father and Button were staggering up the path to the house, helping a man who was stumbling between them. The man had a soldier's uniform on, but the uniform was torn, dirty, and bloody. The man's head rolled to the side, and Celeste could see that his face was bruised and swollen.

"Tom!" screamed Lilly and nearly fell down the steps trying to reach her menfolk.

Somehow they got Tom inside the house and laid on a bed. Shaking off feelings of anger, panic, and fear, Celeste quickly got her brother's uniform and shirt off, and with practiced fingers probed the bruised and bloody body. Tom groaned as she touched his side. Lilly was sobbing behind her, and Samuel was saying, "Now, hold on, Lilly... there, there, don't cry so... he home; he safe."

Celeste looked up at her grief-stricken parents and a wide-eyed Button. "Mostly cuts and bruises—but I think his ribs are broken again. Button, get me some soap and hot water. Mama, I need a clean sheet torn into some long bandages. Papa, where's that medicine Dr. Jackson gave you for pain?"

Half an hour later, Celeste came out of the room and shut the door softly behind her. "I think he'll sleep awhile now." She went over to her father, who was sitting wearily in a chair at the table. "Papa? *What happened?*"

Between Samuel and Button, the story came out in pieces. They'd been walking home from Williams' blacksmith shop, going slow because of Samuel's limp, when they heard shouts, grunts, curses, and thuds in an alleyway between two houses, like a fight was going on. Samuel was going to hurry Button on by and not get involved, when he heard one of the men grunt angrily, "Huh! Uppity nigger boy thinks he's so smart, wearing that uniform."

Another laughed. "That'll teach 'im not to walk around here like he's as good as any white man."

A third man joined in. "Yeah. He thinks the Germans were bad? Ha. Now he's dealin' with the Klan."

Samuel had pulled Button back into the shadows behind a shed until the three white fellows had sauntered on by. Then father and son had moved quickly into the alleyway and knelt beside the crumpled figure on the ground.

"It was—" Samuel Key's voice broke.

"It was Tom!" finished Button. "He wasn't out cold, though. When he saw it was us, he mumbled somethin' 'bout gettin' in on the afternoon train, didn't know how to let us know he was comin', so he just thought he'd surprise us."

For a long while, the family just sat together at the table in wounded silence. Finally Samuel spoke aloud all their thoughts.

"I sent my boy to war. He fought for his country. Lord spared him, thank God! Only... only to come home to another war in our own backyard."

"Lord have mercy!" whispered Lilly, her crying finally spent.

Celeste stood up, her face unsmiling and determined. "Oh, Mama. There was one more thing I had to tell you. Mrs. Bethune is sure that Congress is going to give women the right to vote—very soon. She wants me to bring you and all the other women we can round up to the civics classes up at the school." Celeste put her hands on the table and leaned forward, her eyes flashing. "We don't have bullets, but we have *ballots*. Every member of this family is going to vote, and vote again, until we get things changed around here!"

✧ ✧ ✧ ✧

Celeste had never been so busy in her life. She worked a full shift at the hospital six days a week. Three nights a week the choir practiced in Faith Hall, and they gave a "Community Concert" on Sunday afternoons. In the rest of her "spare" time, she and Mrs. Bethune and others went knocking on doors, encouraging both men and women to come to the evening classes at Daytona Educational and Industrial Institute. Celeste felt a surge of satisfaction when, after years of brushing it off, her mother signed up for reading, writing, and civics.

One day Mrs. Bethune came back from town with a big grin, waving a newspaper. **WOMEN GET THE VOTE!** shouted the headlines. It was dated August 18, 1920. "This will double our voter pool," Mrs. Bethune said eagerly. "And there's a local election here in Daytona this fall. Now we can get a petition for electricity and sewers for Shanty Town onto the ballot. And *then*," she smiled broadly, "we need to get out the vote!"

Celeste and others worked feverishly to register voters as the date of the election grew closer. She was glad she had choir practice and the Sunday afternoon concerts in the school auditorium to keep her spirit calm and joyful and centered on the Lord.

A week before the election, Mrs. Bethune announced that she had to take a trip up to Jacksonville to make a presentation about the school to some potential donors.

"But, Mrs. Bethune," Celeste protested. "The election is important! You can't leave now."

Mrs. Bethune smiled reassuringly. "I'll be back the day before the election. Don't worry. It's all in God's hands."

But Celeste was nervous. Ever since Tom's beating, she felt tension as she walked through town, politely greeting people. Who was a friend? Who was a foe?

Gossip was flying. Men in general were shaking their heads. Women voting, indeed! What was the world coming to? But underneath, there were other murmurs: People were unhappy with how many of the colored folks—men and women—were registering to vote. Couldn't let that happen. It upset the balance of things.

Still, the election was two days away and nothing had happened. Celeste was glad for choir practice that night. She worked the younger students hard, perfecting one of her favorite songs: "My soul has been anchored . . . anchored in the Lord!" *That's right,* she said to herself after practice as she went around Faith Hall and turned off the lights. *That's where I need to keep my focus—anchored in the Lord.*

She had just turned off the last light and was

about to go out and lock the door behind her when she saw flickers of firelight coming down the road. Peering out a darkened window, she could make out people on horseback, clothed in white robes and hoods, and carrying torches. The torches turned off Second Avenue and came up the drive toward Faith Hall.

Cold chills ran up and down Celeste's spine. It was happening... happening again. Were they going to burn down the school? Should she run? Sound the alarm? But she felt frozen, as if nailed to the floor.

She watched, frightened, as two men dismounted. It looked like they were digging a hole with a shovel. The other horsemen, ghostly white in the moonlight, milled about. One was giving orders. More strange movements; they were sticking something in the hole, like a fence post. A clink of a can... a flash of light... and suddenly the crossed beams of the "fence post" burst into flames. And then Celeste knew what it was.

A burning cross.

The men mounted again, their horses wheeling and snorting nervously around the fire. Then, with whoops and yells, their torches still blazing, the white-robed figures rode back the way they had come.

Celeste slowly sank to the floor beside the window and wept with relief that nothing worse had happened. But when the tears slowed, the fear returned. It was a warning. Would they come back the next night? What if they didn't stop with a burning cross and burned down the school?

✧ ✧ ✧ ✧

When Mrs. Bethune returned from her trip the next day, she was met by anxious students and sober teachers. Even though the charred cross had been quickly dismantled and taken away by teachers the next morning, the parched grass and smell of kerosene lingered as a stark reminder.

"What are we going to do?" asked Frances Keyser. She was the practical one, Mrs. Bethune's right hand. "Should we ask some of the neighbor men to stand guard tonight?"

"Yes! Yes!" chorused some of the girls fearfully.

Celeste worked up her courage to speak. "Maybe—maybe we shouldn't vote tomorrow. Tell people to stay home. These people mean business! They'll come back... they will! I know it because... because..." Her voice faltered. The memory of her father's blacksmith shop burning to the ground was too painful.

Mrs. Bethune's strong arms went around Celeste's shoulders. "That's the very reason we have to vote tomorrow. If we don't, they'll come back again and again and again. We have to take a stand. Now. Here." She looked around at the anxious students and teachers. "Mrs. Keyser, take a team of girls and teachers and contact every voter that we've registered. Tell them to meet here at the school at eight o'clock sharp tomorrow morning."

She turned to Celeste. "Is tonight choir practice?"

"No," said Celeste, swallowing hard. "Last night."

"Well, it's choir practice again tonight! Hear that, everyone? Tonight, Faith Hall. The *whole school.*"

✧ ✧ ✧ ✧

Dusk faded to darkness, and the whole school gathered in Faith Hall for choir practice.

Celeste pulled Mrs. Bethune aside. "Shouldn't we turn out the lights? Or at least pull the curtains. Surely we don't want them to know we're all together in one building."

Mrs. Bethune smiled calmly. "Exactly the opposite. Turn on the lights—*all* the lights! Evil deeds love darkness rather than light. We will stand in the light."

Soon lights shone from every room on all four floors of Faith Hall, flooding the driveway, grass, and flower beds around the main building with cheerful welcome. Breathing a prayer to still her pounding heart, Celeste got the girls' attention. "Let's begin with a traditional spiritual—one we all know." Soon the beautiful strains were filling the room.

Not my brother, not my sister,
But it's me, O Lord,
Standing in the need of prayer....

Meanwhile, Mary Bethune positioned herself at the bottom of the steps leading up to the large front porch of Faith Hall, leaving the front door wide open. Crickets joined the chorus floating from the windows.

It's me, O Lord,
Standing in the need of prayer.

And then the ghost riders came. Torches leaping, horses champing nervously, the small posse turned off Second Avenue and rode up the school drive. But the white-robed figures seemed confused by all the lights pouring from Faith Hall and the imposing figure calmly waiting for them on the steps, and they stopped at the far edge of the pool of light.

Two men dismounted, and Mrs. Bethune heard the clank of a kerosene can bumping wooden beams. The men in the shadows hesitated, then turned back to argue in low undertones with the lead man on horseback.

Cursing, the man on horseback yelled out, "We hear you're teaching colored folks around here to vote!" The voice sounded suspiciously like a certain city councilman.

Mrs. Bethune's voice was strong and clear. "We teach civics, if that's what you mean—the rights and responsibilities of every citizen of this great country."

The little group seemed to be arguing among themselves, moving nervously just beyond the light. Then the leader yelled out again, "This is a warning!

Don't bring your people to vote tomorrow, or we'll burn your school to the ground!"

Just then a new song burst from the windows of Faith Hall and seemed to pierce the night....

My soul has been anchored,
Anchored in the Lord!
No man can harm me....

Mary Bethune yelled back, "You can hear our answer. If you burn this school to the ground, we'll build it up again. And if you burn it a second time, we'll build it again and again and again!"

As the gospel music floated from the windows behind her, the men on foot dropped their armloads and hastily remounted their horses. Soon hoofbeats and torches were disappearing into the night.

Mrs. Bethune walked down the drive and stood looking at the two beams of wood and the unused can of kerosene lying where they'd been dumped. She picked up the can. "Hmm," she murmured. "Guess they didn't want this. We can always use an extra can of kerosene."

Chapter 13

One Hundred Strong

THE NEXT MORNING DAWNED bright, warm, and clear. Gentle sea breezes moved the tops of the palms. Spanish moss dripping from the huge oak trees swayed in a lovely dance.

People on foot seemed to be pouring from both directions on Second Avenue and turning into the driveway of the school. Men and women carrying babies, skipping children, lanky young men making eyes at the girls dressed in their Sunday best—on and on they came.

Tears of joy misted Celeste's eyes as she saw her parents come slowly up the drive, Samuel Key leaning on his cane. She blinked rapidly, then realized Button and Buddy were horsing around behind them, and beyond them Lucy and her husband, carrying their little girl, all dressed up in pink frills and pink bows in her hair.

And then she saw Tom—dressed up in his cleaned and mended uniform of the United States Army.

As the group gathered in front of Faith Hall, Mrs. Bethune called for attention and asked, "How many registered voters have we got here?"

Hands were raised—lots and lots of hands. To Celeste's astonishment, she saw Buddy, Tom, Lucy, and her husband raise their hands, too. The teachers counted. "...ninety-eight, ninety-nine, one hundred—and more!" crowed Frances Keyser.

Cheers, laughter, and hats were thrown into the air.

"All right, then, let's go!" said Mrs. Bethune happily.

The crowd surged back down the drive toward town. A song was begun, and voices lifted in praise.

Done made my vow to the Lord,
And I never will turn back.
I will go, I shall go,
To see what the end will be.

Celeste caught up with her family. "When did you turn twenty-one?" she hissed in Buddy's ear.

"When you weren't lookin'!" he teased.

"Tom? How—? When—?"

Her older brother nodded soberly. "Learned to read in the army—they had classes. Didn't tell you. Didn't care—when I got home and met my 'welcoming committee,' I mean. But . . ." He shrugged. "Something Mrs. Bethune said once set me to thinkin'. She said, 'The white man has been thinking for us too long. We want him to think *with* us instead of *for* us.' Guess if I don't vote, I be lettin' him keep doin' my thinkin' for me."

Celeste smiled and took her brother's arm. She swung along in happy silence for awhile, and then as the singing crowd turned down Main Street, she lifted her voice.

. . . I never will turn back.
I will go, I shall go
To see what the end will be.

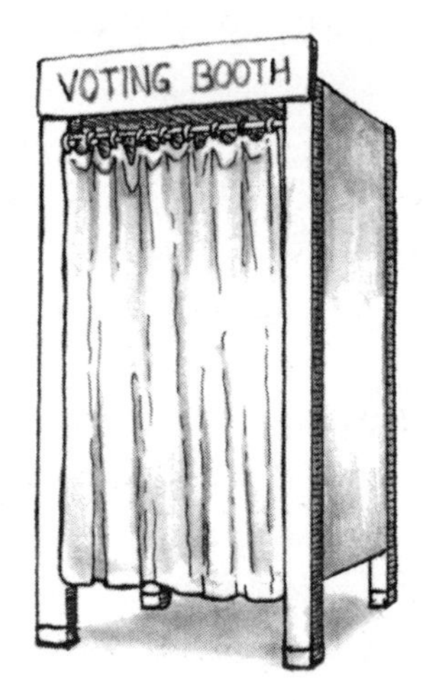

More About Mary McLeod Bethune

IN 1776, THE SCHOONER *Millicent* left the coast of Africa for North America. On board was a living cargo of captured slaves, including a young woman, daughter of an African ruler, and her husband. To her despair, her husband died during the voyage.

In the new land, the young woman was sold as a slave to a rice plantation near Charleston, South Carolina. Totally cut off from her former life—country, language, food, relatives, culture, status—everything was changed. The former princess was nothing more than someone's property.

That was the same year that the Declaration of Independence was penned: "We hold these truths to be self-evident, that all men are created equal, that they are endowed by their Creator with certain unalienable Rights, that among these are Life, Liberty, and the pursuit of Happiness...." But to avoid controversy, the revolutionaries who were demanding their own freedom from England left out a proposed clause condemning slavery.

Ninety-nine years later, in 1875, a little girl was born—the great-granddaughter of that African princess. The fifteenth child of Sam and Patsy McLeod, former slaves who had been freed by the Emancipation Proclamation of 1863, she was named Mary. After generations of servitude, she was *born free*.

But life was hard for the McLeods. They bought a small parcel of land from their former master and raised cotton, barely scratching out a living from the land near Mayesville, South Carolina. And then one day a light-skinned Negro woman came to call. Her name was Miss Wilson, and she was starting a mission school. Could the McLeods send their children?

School? *Miss* Wilson? To be educated and respected like the white folks? It was a new day for the McLeod family.

They decided that eleven-year-old Mary should go. She was "plain but smart." After three years of schooling, she helped teach other children to read, and even white folks came to her to help them do "figuring" (arithmetic).

Then in 1889, Mary Crissman, a Quaker woman in Colorado, wrote to Scotia Seminary in Concord, North Carolina, and said she would like to pay for the schooling of a colored girl "who would make good." Scotia had been established by the Presbyterian Church for the education of "daughters of freedmen." Miss Wilson, an alumnus of Scotia, recommended Mary McLeod.

Scotia was a life-changing experience. Two white teachers crumbled Mary's stereotypes about all white people wanting to "keep the Negro in his place." These teachers cared about her as a person. She studied literature, Latin, Greek, Bible, and American democracy—and made them her own. During her Scotia years, Mary decided she wanted to become a missionary to Africa, to her own people.

At twenty, Mary graduated from Scotia, and went to Moody Bible Institute to prepare to be a missionary. On the way, she encountered Jim Crow laws and had to ride in a separate train car from whites.

After graduation from Moody, she was told by the Presbyterian mission board that they had "no openings for a colored missionary to Africa." Many years later, Mary McLeod described it as "the greatest disappointment of my life."

But never one to give up or hold a grudge, Mary turned disappointment into challenge. She would become a teacher to her own people right here in the South. She became convinced that education was the key to equality between blacks and whites. She was glad that black colleges were being established—but how could the children of the South go to college if they didn't even know how to read?

Years later Carrie Walker said to her, "What our people need is a few millionaires. Before I die

I'm going to make a million dollars." Mary McLeod Bethune replied, "I'd rather make a million readers."

Mary taught at Haines Institute in Augusta, Georgia, then Kendall Institute in Sumter. And a dream began to grow to establish her own school, a school that would teach children who otherwise had no opportunity. And this was the dream:

1. She'd fill it with song—not just for getting money but to express the longings of her people.
2. It would look like Scotia—beautiful grounds.
3. It would train boys and girls to work for a living at all sorts of skilled trades and farming.
4. It would also give all the world's learning. To her, vocational training included not only the technique of actual work but intelligent comprehension of one's duties as a citizen and the ability to partake of the higher spiritual life of this world.
5. It would teach the duties (and privileges!) of citizenship.
6. It would be a living part of the community—that is, it would educate and support people to do something about the Jim Crow laws and the lynchings; it would keep people voting.

At Kendall Institute she met another teacher, Albertus Bethune, and they were married in May, 1898, when Mary was twenty-three. When their child, Albert, was born, Mary stayed home "one precious year" to care for the baby. But the dream would not die.

The Bethunes were teaching in Palatka, Florida, when Mary heard about the railroad workers who were building the Florida East Coast Railroad in 1904. Who was educating their children? She decided to visit Daytona Beach, Florida, to find out.

What happened in Daytona Beach is recounted in the story you have just read.

In 1923, the school-on-a-shoestring that Mrs. Mary Bethune had started with five little girls in 1904 merged with Cookman College from Jacksonville, Florida, to become the nationally recognized Bethune-Cookman College. She remained its president, but more and more she was called on to advise leaders and presidents who were concerned about the cause of justice and civil rights for black citizens.

Among her many accomplishments and responsibilities, she joined the Urban League, which worked to get better jobs and better housing for black people, and the National Association for the Advancement of Colored People (NAACP), which battled discrimination and segregation in the courts. In the 1930s, Mrs. Bethune created the National Council of Negro Women and was its president for fourteen years.

In 1933, Franklin D. Roosevelt was elected President of the United States. Both President Roosevelt and his wife, Eleanor, greatly respected Mrs. Bethune and often turned to her for advice. Roosevelt appointed her as "advisor" to the National Youth Administration; eventually she was put in charge of black affairs under the NYA. During this time she also organized the Federal Council of Negro Affairs.

Mary McLeod Bethune worked tirelessly her entire life for the welfare of her people. But she did not bully or insult people who disagreed with her. In 1926, Dr. Hamilton Holt, the president of Rollins College in Flordia, invited her to speak at a student assembly. The board of trustees flatly refused to allow it. Dr. Holt came to Mrs. Bethune with the news, practically in tears, ready to resign his position at this insult to her. "Don't do that," she said. "The students of Florida, both black and white, need you more than anything I have to say next Friday."

Twenty-three years later, the trustees of Rollins College unanimously voted to give Mrs. Mary Bethune an honorary doctorate degree. It was a particularly special honor for Mrs. Bethune, a confirmation of Lincoln's words, "We destroy our enemies when we make them our friends."

After Mrs. Bethune died in 1955, a portion of her will was read to the students of Bethune-Cookman College: "I leave you love.... I leave you hope.... I leave you a thirst for education.... I leave, finally, a responsibility to our young people."

For Further Reading

Meltzer, Milton. *Mary McLeod Bethune: Voice of Black Hope*. A "Women of Our Time" book. New York: Puffin Books (Viking Penquin, Inc.), 1987.

Peare, Catherine Owens. *Mary McLeod Bethune.* New York: The Vanguard Press, Inc., 1951.

Sterne, Emma Gelders. *Mary McLeod Bethune*. New York: Alfred A. Knopf, 1957.

CPSIA information can be obtained
at www.ICGtesting.com
Printed in the USA
LVOW07s1735111217
559405LV00005B/1285/P